OTHER YEARLING BOOKS YOU WILL ENJOY:

HAPPILY EVER AFTER . . . ALMOST, *Judie Wolkoff*
WHAT DO YOU DO WHEN YOUR MOUTH WON'T OPEN?,
Susan Beth Pfeffer
COURAGE, DANA, *Susan Beth Pfeffer*
ANASTASIA AGAIN!, *Lois Lowry*
ANASTASIA, ASK YOUR ANALYST, *Lois Lowry*
ANASTASIA HAS THE ANSWERS, *Lois Lowry*
ANASTASIA ON HER OWN, *Lois Lowry*
ANASTASIA AT YOUR SERVICE, *Lois Lowry*
BLUBBER, *Judy Blume*
ARE YOU THERE GOD? IT'S ME, MARGARET., *Judy Blume*

YEARLING BOOKS/YOUNG YEARLINGS/YEARLING CLASSICS are designed especially to entertain and enlighten young people. Patricia Reilly Giff, consultant to this series, received her bachelor's degree from Marymount College. She holds a master's degree in history from St. John's University, and a Professional Diploma in Reading from Hofstra University. She was a teacher and reading consultant for many years, and is the author of numerous books for young readers.

For a complete listing of all Yearling titles, write to
Dell Readers Service, P.O. Box 1045,
South Holland, IL 60473.

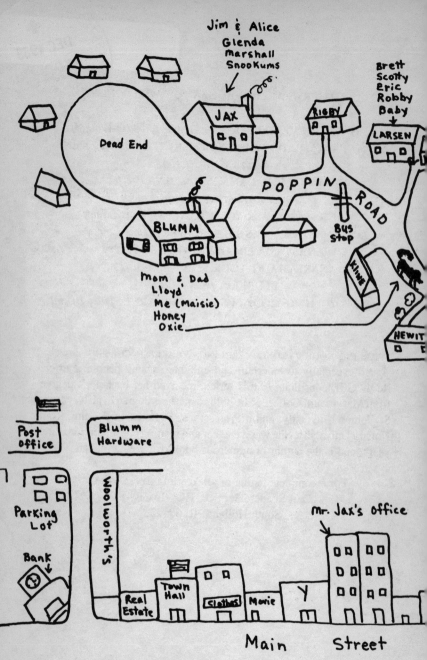

The Town of Deer Creek
by Maisie Blumm

JUDIE WOLKOFF
In·A·Pig's·Eye

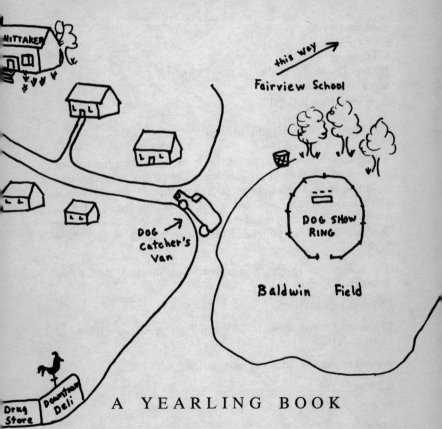

A YEARLING BOOK

J
W

Published by
Dell Publishing
a division of
Bantam Doubleday Dell Publishing Group, Inc.
666 Fifth Avenue
New York, New York 10103

ISBN: 0-440-40140-2

Reprinted by arrangement with Bradbury Press, an Affiliate of Macmillan, Inc.

Printed in the United States of America

February 1989

10 9 8 7 6 5 4 3 2

CW

This book is dedicated to friendship.
with love and affection to two special
friends of mine . . .

CAROLE—
who helped me pass algebra,
survive Cheyenne, and enjoy IFHS, biology,
Mexico, and our *grand* reunion.

JANET—
wise, funny, thoughtful,
unparalleled in her knowledge of
sports trivia, true-blue,
and *always* there.

JW

◆ Chapter 1 ◆

THE CLASSROOM was unusually quiet except for the soft, constant scratching of pencils moving across lined notebook paper. Maisie sighed and flexed her cramped fingers. For the last quarter of an hour, she'd been writing non-stop to someone she'd never met, spilling out everything she thought was important to tell about herself. Had she forgotten anything?

She pushed up the sleeves of her pale blue cotton sweater, rested her elbows on her desk, and read over the letter she'd written.

March 16
65 Poppin Road
Deer Creek, Connecticut

Dear whoever finds this,
*   The person writing to you is me, Maisie (May-zee) Blumm, with two m's. I'm 10, 67 pounds and short,*

*but not so short I have to worry or take growing pills.
I've got brown eyes, brown hair that kinks up if it's
not blow-dried, and I hate shrimp. My best friend
used to be Glenda Jax. She's still nine and she has
dirty blond hair. When we're standing back to back,
she's taller. But when we're sitting, I am. (Glenda's
all legs.) I stopped liking her on the school bus this
morning. She was a real jerk.*

*Glenda has a Yorkshire terrier named Snookums
and a brother, Marshall. Marshall is 7. He takes
peewee karate lessons at the Y with my sister, Honey.
Honey's 8 and thinks she's tough. We all live on
Poppin Road. It's a dead-end street with sixteen families. The Jaxes' house is yellow. Ours is white with
blue shutters.*

*Two years ago my family got a dog. Somebody left
him on purpose in my dad's hardware store. His
name is Oxie and he's real smart, no matter what
Glenda, the jerk, said about him on the bus. My
brother Lloyd thinks Oxie is mostly shepherd, but I
don't. I think he's got sheep dog in him and a lot of
husky. You can see the husky in his tail. It's curly like
this*

*Lloyd's 14. He's not getting his allowance this
week. (You'd know why if you saw his room.) Every
other word he says is* like. *It drives my mom crazy.*

*But his rock music gets on everybody's nerves. In
May I'm putting Oxie in the Deer Creek Dog Show.
He'll be in two categories. Best Trick and Most
Beautiful. Deer Creek is where I live. My address is
at the top.*

*These are my hobbies:—dressing up, putting on
skits, teaching Oxie new tricks, using my dad's binoc-
ulars, and making marshmallow krispies. I stopped
playing my recorder. The plastic gave my tongue can-
chors. When I grow up I want to be a famous animal
trainer. Either that or a spy or a newspaper pub-
lisher.*

*This is being sent on a balloon so it can't be more
than one page. It's okay if I write on both sides,
though. When you find it, please write me a long letter. . . .*

Maisie bit the eraser on her pencil, wondering
if she should cross out what she said about
Glenda. Well, maybe not. Glenda *had* been a
jerk! She'd started the fight. But if they made
up and became friends again, then what? Was
there a chance Glenda would ever find out what
was in the letter?

"Boys and girls . . ."

Naw. It'd be impossible, Maisie decided. The
letter was going to sail away on a balloon. Glenda
would never know what it said. Not in a billion
years.

"Boys and girls . . . *please*. I need your attention."

Along with everyone else in her fourth-grade class, Maisie looked up at Miss Lange, the teacher.

"We're due out in the ballfield for send-off in fifteen minutes," Miss Lange said. "So let's finish our letters quickly. Which reminds me . . . did you all tell about our special occasion?"

Maisie pulled her pencil out of her mouth and began writing as fast as she could.

Sorry this part's sloppy, but I forgot to tell you that my school is having a birthday. It's ten years old today. To celebrate, we're sending up 572 balloons. They'll all have letters.

Your friend,

Maisie Blumm

P.S. If Glenda takes back what she said about Oxie, I'll take back what I said about Snookums looking like a hairy mouse. Even if she does.

This is Snookums

·Chapter 2·

MAISIE was sure the noise in the field could be heard as far away as the heart of Africa.

Five hundred seventy-two children, all talking and shouting, had formed a circle around the boundaries of the baseball diamond. Above each child's head was a helium balloon tugging at the end of a string. Attached to each balloon was a personal letter, safely sealed inside a plastic sandwich bag.

Maisie's balloon was bright green, the color of the Granny Smith apple she'd eaten for lunch. She'd wanted yellow, then changed her mind because she was sure yellow was the color Glenda would choose. And she was right. When her class passed Glenda's going out to the field, that's what Glenda was carrying—a yellow balloon.

Glenda didn't speak to Maisie. And Maisie didn't speak to Glenda. They were still ex-best friends.

"I want my balloon to land on a Coast Guard

ship," Steven was saying to Jason. "Where do you want yours to land?"

Jason, the tallest boy in Miss Lange's class, thumped Steven on the head. "On Jupiter. Where else?"

Maisie clamped her fingers tighter around the string in her hand and raised herself on tiptoes to look over Jason's shoulder. Dr. Scotch, the school principal, was standing on home plate. As he waited for everyone to quiet down, the flaps on his brown suit jacket snapped in the strong March wind. Maisie thought he looked cold. She was. And she hoped Glenda was freezing.

"Boys, girls . . . members of the faculty," Dr. Scotch shouted into his bullhorn, "ten years ago today, Fairview School opened its doors to students for the first time. Though most of you are too young to remember that historic occasion, we are all, in some way, indebted to the many services our school has provided. And now, on Fairview's birthday, we want to share our celebration. Are you ready for send-off?"

"*Yes!!*" shouted five hundred seventy-two children, who were also glad his speech was over.

"Good!" shouted Dr. Scotch. "At the count of three, we'll begin by singing, 'Happy Birthday.' As we finish, I'll raise my hand, giving you the signal to release your balloons. Afterward we'll all return to the building for birthday cake. Ready?"

"*Yes!*"

"One, two . . ."

There was a chorus of gasps. A red balloon had shot up into the air! Someone in second grade hadn't listened. In unison, Maisie's entire fourth-grade class turned their heads, looking for the culprit.

"Three!" said Dr. Scotch.

"Happy birthday to youuuuuu," sang the group assembled on the field, "Happy birthday toooo you. Happy birthday, dear Fairview . . ." Every eye followed the truant red balloon as it sailed high over a grove of Canadian hemlocks. "Happy birthday to youuuuu!"

Dr. Scotch was giving the signal. It was time. The moment every boy and girl (but one) had waited for. Send-off!

Up went the balloons.

As if by magic, the somber, gray March sky became as bright as a Dutch tulip garden. Maisie rubbed her cold hands together, watching the peaceful explosion of color. Her eyes stayed fixed on her green balloon until it was no bigger than a speck of confetti.

Soon there was no trace of color left in the sky. The balloons were on their way.

"Time for us to head back to the building," said Miss Lange.

Her fourth-grade class was one of the last to leave the ballfield. As Maisie walked behind Jason and Steven, she felt a little shiver of excitement wondering how far her balloon would travel. Maybe it would reach Hollywood. And a famous movie star would find it and send her a letter.

Maisie beamed. Boy, wouldn't *that* make Glenda jealous!

But even if her balloon didn't make it to Hollywood, she could think of dozens of other good places where it might go. To Paris, for instance. Or Mexico. Or head far north and be picked up by someone who raised reindeer. Or cross the Great Lakes and . . .

"You know what I'll bet?" Jason said to Steven. "Half these balloons are going to get caught in trees."

Steven laughed. "Yeah! Trees right here in Deer Creek."

Maisie nearly tripped going up the stairs behind him. That couldn't happen! *Or could it?*

By now all the children were back in school, either coming out of the lunchroom with cake, or going in there for some. Maisie's class was on its way in, but she wasn't thinking of anything as good as cake. She was imagining her balloon getting tangled in Glenda's crab apple tree. And *Glenda* finding her letter.

"Hey! Watch it!"

Maisie was too late. Red punch had spilled down the front of a sixth-grade boy who was holding a paper cup in one hand and a piece of cake in the other. It was Benedict, who rode her bus. And she'd walked right into him. "I'm sorry, Benedict . . . I didn't see you," she said.

"Didn't *see* me?" Benedict shoved his cake in his mouth and dabbed at his shirt with his napkin. "Wait! I know you . . . you're Maisie-Daisy, the girl with that dingbat dog."

"Uh-uh, not me," she said, backing off. "You're thinking of Glenda. *She's* the one with the Yorkie. My dog's a husky."

"A *husky*?"

"Well, part of him is."

"Oh, yeah?" Benedict started laughing. "Which part . . . his tonsils?"

Maisie had a funny feeling that maybe Benedict had seen Oxie. She couldn't get away from him fast enough and spun on her heels, disappearing with her class as it filed into the crowded lunchroom.

HAPPY BIRTHDAY TO THE BEST SCHOOL IN THE UNIVERSE, said a sign some fifth-graders had taped over the double doors.

"Still smells of tuna fish chow mein in here," Steven announced in a loud voice as the class entered.

"Yeah, last *month's* chow mein," Jason added, even louder.

Miss Lange shot the two boys a sharp, better-behave-yourselves look, then led the class through the stuffy room toward two tables set up in the center. Laid across them was a beautiful, enormous white birthday cake decorated with countless pink and yellow sugar rosebuds. In the middle were the words HAPPY TENTH BIRTHDAY, FAIRVIEW SCHOOL, written in thick streams of dark chocolate.

"Over here, please," said Miss Lange, indicating where she wanted the class to line up.

A third of the cake was already gone. Parent volunteers, standing at each of the four corners, had sliced it up and passed it out, along with cups of fruit punch. What was left, however, was still impressive.

Maisie stood in line at the tail end of her class, listening to a group of little first-graders *oohing* and *ahhing* over the size of the cake.

"I think it was baked in the White House!" said one.

"Not me," said another.

"Where then?"

"In a *giant's* oven."

Maisie smiled to herself because she knew the truth. Her mother had been on the PTA baking committee. The cake was actually thirty-five individual sheet cakes frosted and decorated so perfectly, not a single seam showed.

"Hi, Maisie. It's me!"

Maisie turned and saw her little sister, Honey, grinning up at her with a red fruit punch mustache. "It's me!" Honey said again, as if they hadn't seen each other in centuries. "I've been through the line already."

"Yeah, I know," said Maisie.

"How?"

"Never mind. Just wipe your mouth."

"You still mad at Glenda?"

Maisie nodded. "Yes. And I always will be."

"She's still mad at you, too. I just asked her," said Honey. "She's over there." Honey pointed toward Mr. Bingham's fourth-grade class on the opposite side of the cake. "See? There's Glenda. Right next to Amy Gooch."

Maisie shrugged. "Doesn't bother me."

"It should. Amy's her best friend now," said Honey. "They're playing together this weekend."

When Maisie glanced across the cake again, she felt stung to the core. This weekend was supposed to be special. She and Glenda had planned to start their very own neighborhood newspaper. *The Poppin Road Gazette*, they were going to call it. And they'd had their hearts set on it for days. But now . . .

"Here you go, dear."

Maisie suddenly realized she was at the front of her line. A parent volunteer smiled, handing her a piece of cake with a plump yellow rosebud. "Don't forget your punch," she added.

Maisie bit her lip as she took it. She wasn't in the mood for punch now. Or cake. But if she walked away empty-handed after she'd stood in line all that time, she'd look like a . . . what was that word her big brother Lloyd always used? A *bimbo*!

Honey was gone. She'd lined up next to Marshall Jax, Glenda's little brother, with their second-grade class. Maisie watched them file out of the lunchroom, then made a beeline for the green rubber trash barrel by the door and flung in her cake. She would have pitched in her punch, too, but she knew the school rule: No liquids in the garbage.

She had to drink it.

Ugh. Warm and much too sweet. A lot like that awful concoction she and Glenda once made with paprika and mouthwash. The last swallow of punch was the worst—like getting down a shoe. When

she finished, she threw her empty cup in the barrel and walked away wishing she were anywhere—absolutely *anywhere*—but here in school.
Nothing, she thought, could beat the misery of
being the *only* unhappy person at the Fairview
School birthday party.

And Maisie was convinced that she was.

BUT NO MORE than Marshall Jax was convinced
that *he* was.

At three o'clock, when the children who rode
Bus 5 were boarding to go home, Marshall slumped
into a seat by the window with his head down and
his hands shoved deep inside the pockets of his
red jacket. He was mad. Mad at Dr. Scotch, his
teacher . . . at nearly everybody but Honey.

Honey, who knew why he was mad, sat down
next to him. "Has anybody on the bus teased
you?" she whispered.

"Not yet," said Marshall.

Honey squinched up her eyes. "If they do," she
said, getting her hands ready for combat, "I'll
karate-chop their heads off!"

When Maisie boarded the bus a few minutes
later, she looked right past them, trying to decide
where to sit. A seat was vacant next to Glenda in
the rear, but Maisie wasn't taking it. Nope. Not

next to Amy Gooch's best friend. Not on her life.

"Come on, move! Mush, mush . . . like your sled dog!" said somebody behind her.

Benedict! Maisie jumped as if she'd been touched by a ghost and went scurrying into a seat across the aisle from Honey and Marshall. Here it comes, she thought. Another smart-aleck remark about Oxie.

But Benedict surprised her. He strolled on by without saying a word.

Whew. Maisie let out her breath. Then she turned and looked—*really* looked—at Honey and Marshall.

Marshall had slid down in his seat so far he looked like a cushion, and Honey was perched on the edge of hers, wildly whacking the air with her hands.

"Hey! Stop that!" said Maisie.

Honey kept whacking. "I can't. I'm protecting Marshall."

Maisie lurched forward as the bus pulled out of the school driveway. "Why? Who's after him?"

"Kids. They're gonna tease him."

"About what?"

"His red balloon." Honey's hands flopped on her lap. *"You mean you didn't see it?"* she screeched. *"Marshall was the one who let go before he was supposed to!"*

As her voice traveled, so did Marshall. He crawled all the way under his seat.

"I'm never going to school again. Ever!" he called. "I *hate* Dr. Scotch!"

"Why's he mad at Dr. Scotch?" asked Maisie.

"For mixing him up," said Honey.

"How'd he mix him up?"

Honey, who wasn't sure herself, leaned down looking at Marshall. "Tell Maisie how Dr. Scotch mixed you up."

"Because," hollered Marshall from the floor of the bus, "he said, 'ready!' too soon. *Before* he counted to three."

"He meant get ready for counting," said Maisie.

"Then he should've said so," said Honey.

"That's right! Then I would've waited," said Marshall, "and nobody'd be teasing me."

"Nobody *is* teasing you," said Maisie.

Honey swiveled her head around to make sure. "She's right, Marsh. They don't dare. I'd whack 'em up!"

Marshall backed out cautiously from under his seat. "You sure?"

Honey crossed her heart. "Now get back up here," she said, picking off a dirty cupcake wrapper that was stuck to his rear end.

"And quit worrying," said Maisie.

As the bus stopped for a red light at an intersection, Honey watched Maisie slump down in her seat, chewing her thumbnail. Talk about worried! Maisie was the one who looked worried. And Honey knew why.

"Want to know a secret, Maze?" she said, crossing the aisle to whisper in Maisie's ear. "Glenda was in the girls' room crying before school got out. I saw her."

"So? She's not my friend anymore."

"That's why she was crying," said Honey. "She wants to move away if you won't be her friend. Her *best* friend."

"I thought Amy Gooch was. They're playing together this weekend."

"Uh-uh. I fibbed," said Honey. "Glenda told me to tell you that so you'd hurry and make up. She wants to work on the newspaper with you."

"Then she shouldn't have said all those mean things about Oxie!"

The light changed to green and Honey scooted back across the aisle to her seat. "They weren't mean, they were true. Oxie *is* silly-looking . . . everybody in the world knows that! And he *is* dumb! But I don't care," she said with a big, wide grin. "I love him anyway."

WHEN the bus made its stop on Poppin Road, Maisie hurried to get off ahead of everyone, but she didn't race home. She stood at the bottom of the steps, waiting for Glenda. Darn, she thought as she shifted her heavy book bag. What's taking her so long?

Glenda was being deliberately pokey. And when she came down the steps, she looked a little red-eyed.

"Hi," said Maisie.

Glenda looked behind her, then back at Maisie. "You mean *me*?"

Maisie nodded and Glenda fiddled with her jacket zipper.

"Umm . . ."

"Yeah?"

"Well, if you're not doing anything, we can go to my house," said Maisie.

"And make marshmallow krispies?"

"Sure. And Shirley Temples. We've got ginger ale and maraschino cherries."

"How about making mouthwash and paprika?"

Maisie giggled. "I know what made you think of that . . . the school punch."

"Eww, yech," said Glenda. "Wasn't it sick?"

"Gross!"

"Disgusting!"

They started up the hill together, talking as fast as they could about the balloons, the send-off, the cake, their letters—everything except their fight that morning.

Then finally Glenda said, "I'm sorry, Maisie . . . I didn't mean those things I said about Oxie. He's not a dumb baboon. And he doesn't really look part squirrel."

"He sort of does," said Maisie.

"His tail, maybe, but not the rest of him. Not enough to keep him out of the dog show."

"And you can definitely enter Snookums as a dog," said Maisie. "The judges won't thing she's a hairy mouse."

"Well . . ."

Maisie shook her head. "Naw. She's just little. And I *like* her color."

When they got to Maisie's house, they saw her mother at the end of the driveway, getting the mail out of the mailbox. "How was school?" she called.

"Great," both girls answered together.

·Chapter 3·

"DROP IT, Oxie!"

As soon as Oxie heard Maisie's command, he clamped his jaws tighter around the corner of her comforter, dragged it off the bed, then streaked out her door and down the stairs with Maisie and Glenda following him in hot pursuit.

"Mom! Honey! Lloyd! Somebody help us!" Maisie hollered. "Oxie's got my new comforter again."

Mrs. Blumm popped out of the kitchen and Honey ran out of the den, asking, "Which way'd he go?" But Lloyd stayed upstairs in his room listening to rock music.

Boom boom, betcha ma baby's sweet bam boom
Ya ever seen her feet bam boom . . .

Each beat sent a tremor through the house.
"Oxie's in the dining room," said Glenda.

She and Maisie dashed in there from one direction, Mrs. Blumm and Honey from the other. Sure enough, Oxie was hiding under the table, sprawled flat across Maisie's new yellow flowered comforter. His tail thumped the floor like he was beating a bongo. This was his favorite game.

"Okay! We gotcha!" said Honey.

Oxie perked up his head and held fast to the corner of the comforter. He watched the four of them closing in on him, then sprang out from under the table, knocking two chairs sideways as he made his escape.

There was a mad scramble of feet as they all followed him down the hall. One minute he was there, the next he wasn't. He'd made a sharp turn into the living room, whipping the tail end of Maisie's comforter around the corner behind him.

"Quick! In the living room," shouted Mrs. Blumm. "He's heading behind the couch."

She and Maisie cornered him at one end, Honey and Glenda at the other. The game was up. Oxie was trapped. He let go of the comforter and Maisie made a grab for it. Then he came prancing out from behind the couch, wagging his tail. "Bad boy!" Maisie scolded.

Oxie sat down and raised his right paw.

"Nope. No cookies for you."

He tried both paws.

"I said no, Oxie. *No* cookies!"

He cocked his head to the side as if he'd understood every word she said, then rolled over and played dead.

Honey grinned. "Shoot! Now *why* can't he do that when we tell him to?"

This time when Maisie and Glenda went upstairs they made sure Maisie's door was shut behind them. They spread the comforter on the bed and settled on top, taking the bowl of popcorn and stack of papers they'd left on the floor when they chased after Oxie.

"Okay? Now where were we? I forget," said Glenda.

"Counting," said Maisie.

They started again. During the weekend, they'd accumulated the following items for the first edition of *The Poppin Road Gazette*:

One short article on world events
National news
Two riddles, one joke, and one maze
A half-page report on Fairview School's birthday
    party
Drawings
An announcement for the upcoming Deer Creek
    Dog Show
Unscramble these words: Pppnio doaR Getzate

Maisie flopped back against a pillow, chewing

popcorn. "What else do we need? Some news about our neighborhood?"

"Good idea," said Glenda. "Let's see. . . ." She picked up some popcorn. "We could tell that the Rosens are moving. Their house is for sale. And Bonnie Rigby's got a crush on a high school football player."

"Right. Number Forty-seven. Honey told me."

"And Mrs. Larsen's expecting again."

"She is?" Maisie reached for a pencil and notebook and began writing. "How'd you know that?"

"I saw her at the store yesterday."

"When's the baby due?"

Glenda thought a minute. "Oh, I'd say in about five or six months. Probably the end of . . ."

"August," wrote Maisie. "Anything else?"

"Hmm . . . Marshall and Honey are taking peewee karate lessons."

"And Lloyd finally cleaned his filthy, dirty room," Maisie added.

Glenda watched her write down the last two items. "Excellent," she said. "Now we need to think of a caption. How about . . ." She drummed her fingers on the comforter. "How about 'Things to Know'? Nope. Make it a question . . . 'Did You Know?' "

Maisie wrote DID YOU KNOW? at the top of the page, then she and Glenda went over their other articles one more time. Neither of them was satisfied. *The Poppin Road Gazette* still needed something.

"Darned if I can think of anything," said Maisie.

"Me either," said Glenda.

They decided to sit cross-legged on the bed, close their eyes, and concentrate. They wouldn't even chew popcorn, so they both swallowed what was in their mouths.

Their eyes snapped shut.

> *Cain't eat! Cain't sleep! Oh, no!*
> *Oh, no!*
> *Ya whacked me out with your deceit!*
> *Oh, yeah! Oh, yeah!*

Their eyes snapped open.

> *So I'm cryin' in the kitchen! Yeah! Yeah!*
> *Wooooo-wooo!*

"Lloyd!" screamed Maisie. His rock music had been blasting down the hall for an hour. But she hadn't noticed till now, when she and Glenda needed to concentrate. "Lloyd!" she screamed again. "Turn that dumb stuff off!"

> *Tears in the toaster! Tears in the sink!*
> *Tears in the fryin' pan, now whaddya think?*
> *Oh, woo! Yeah! Yeah!*

"He probably can't hear you," said Glenda.

Maisie hopped off the bed. "Come on," she said.

She and Glenda marched out of her room, down the hall and up three steps to the landing over the garage where Lloyd's room was. She pounded on the door. "Lloyd!" she yelled. "I'm warning you . . . turn it off!"

Cain't eat! Cain't sleep! Ya whacked me out . . .

Maisie pounded harder.

"Maybe something's happened to him," said Glenda. "He could be choking or bleeding or . . ."

Maisie turned the knob and slowly pushed the door open. "Lloyd?"

"Wow!" said Glenda. "I thought he cleaned his room."

"He did," said Maisie. "You should've seen it before."

They stepped over a wet towel, then a sneaker, clumps of underwear, one, two, three socks . . . a plate with a pizza crust, another sock, a soccer shoe, an empty shampoo bottle and several more towels before they made it to a small clearing by Lloyd's bed.

"I guess he showers a lot," said Glenda.

Maisie looked around. "Lloyd? Lloyd, you in here?"

"And he sort of makes his bed."

Maisie poked the lump in the middle. "*Lloyd*?"

"And he must drink tons of sodas. Wow! Cans on his dresser. Cans on his desk. Cans on his . . ." Glenda stepped between a stack of tapes and a bag of potato chips to look at the wall of posters behind Lloyd's desk. "Every rock singer who's ever lived," she said. "You can't even see his wallpaper." Her eyes traveled from the posters to a black box with switches and a green light bleeping across a panel. "What's that?"

Maisie shrugged. "I don't know. I've never seen it."

"Don't you come in here much?"

"Usually you can't."

By now, they'd realized Lloyd wasn't in his room. But they weren't leaving. There were too many interesting things to look at.

"Hey, Maze . . . come here a second. You won't believe this calendar."

Maisie put down a pad of stationery that said, FROM THE DESK OF THE WORLD'S GREATEST HUNK, hopped over an overflowing wastebasket, and sidled up to Glenda.

"See? It's like a book . . . three hundred sixty-five pages. And each one's got a picture of a girl. Look at Miss Fourth of July!" Glenda flipped through the pages near the middle, then stopped. "Isn't that a wicked bikini?"

Maisie giggled. "What's Easter got? A girl in a bunny suit?"

"We're about to find out." Glenda flipped forward to April, then slowed down, turning over a page at a time. Each picture seemed to get funnier. "Nope, wrong," she hooted. "Miss Easter's hatching out of a giant—"

"*Hey!*" The voice shot across the room like a big gun. "*Like what're you bimbos doing?*"

Maisie and Glenda nearly jumped out of their socks. *Lloyd!* Lloyd wearing what Mr. Blumm called his at-home uniform: an oversize, inside-out, cut-up blue sweatshirt and a carpenter's hat. He was munching the end of a foot-long sandwich.

"Like out!" he roared with a full mouth. "Out, out, out!"

"Okay, we will. But first you have to turn off your dumb stereo," said Maisie. "It's so loud we can't think!"

Lloyd scratched under the arm of his cut-up blue sweatshirt. "It *is* off."

"No, it's not! It's—"

"Like off!" he repeated. "Turned off automatically. While I was in the kitchen."

"Good! Keep it off!" Maisie looked down at the floor and made a face as if she were ready to wade through a swamp full of crocodiles. "Careful, Glenda," she said as she took a yard-high step over a towel. "Watch your feet."

Glenda crouched down, ready to broad-jump a sock.

"Not so fast," said Lloyd. "I want my calendar."

"What calendar?" said Maisie.

"You have a calendar?" said Glenda.

Lloyd dropped his sandwich on the dresser and swooped Glenda in the air under her arms.

"Hey! Put her down . . . she's a *guest*!" yelled Maisie.

"Not till I get back my stolen property," Lloyd said, shaking and rattling Glenda until his calendar dropped out from under her sweater.

Maisie watched it land on the floor. "Oh. You meant *that* calendar."

"Yeah, like I meant *that* calendar," he mimicked. "Now, out you go, bambinos . . . both of you. Beat it, scram, *adios*!" He shoved them out the door and slammed it.

Glenda stared at the door as the lock clicked. "Wow! Is *he* rude!"

"Yeah! Who does he think you are?" said Maisie. "Part of our family?"

"I know what I'd do if he was *my* brother," Glenda said as they started down the hall.

"Knock a few of his friends around?"

"Nope. I'd write a letter to that 'Dear Abby' lady. . . ."

Maisie stopped in her tracks. "You mean the one in the paper?"

"Yeah, she gives all kinds of great advice. You know. 'Go to the doctor.' 'Kick the bum out of the house.' Stuff like that. I read her column all the time."

Maisie was off and running. "That's it!" she said. "That's the idea we needed. An advice column."

She was already on the floor of her closet, digging through a carton of odds and ends, when Glenda ran in the room after her. "I know I've got a good piece of oak tag in here somewhere," she said, then came crawling out a second later, holding one up. "Here. This'll be perfect for a poster."

"What's the poster for?" said Glenda.

"To advertise. How else will people find out we have an advice column?"

Glenda sat on the bed. "I don't know, Maze. 'Dear Abby' is probably expensive. Where are we going to get the money to pay her?"

"Not her. *Us!* You and me . . . we'll write it. Only . . ." Maisie sat back on her heels, thinking. "Only we'd better think of a new name. 'Dear Glenda and Maisie' might not get us many letters."

"How about 'Dear Glemaise'?"

Maisie shook her head. "Something totally different. So nobody'll guess it's us."

" 'Dear Uncle Buster'?"

"Hmm." Maisie considered a moment. "Maybe a woman's name would sound better."

"Ruthie, Cornelia, Jane, Susan, Polly . . ."

"Polly! That's good."

Glenda still wasn't satisfied. "How about 'Dear *Aunt* Polly'?"

"Terrific! 'Dear Aunt Polly'!" cried Maisie. "I love it."

FIFTEEN minutes later she and Glenda left the house, heading down the street with a bag of thumbtacks, a hammer, their finished poster, and Oxie trotting close at their heels.

"Where're you guys going?" called Marshall, who was across the street pedaling his blue bike with training wheels.

"Down the hill," answered Glenda. "We're hanging up a very important poster."

"Can I come?"

"Sure. Tell everybody you see to come," called Maisie.

By the time she and Glenda reached the telephone pole near the bus stop—the place where they'd decided to hang their poster—half a dozen younger neighborhood children had joined their procession. Glenda ordered everyone to stand back.

Maisie held the poster against the telephone

pole, then stuck out her hand. "The hammer, please."

With a grand flourish, Glenda placed it in her hand, and with another grand flourish, Maisie pounded in the first thumbtack.

"What's the sign say?" asked Marshall.

Maisie pounded in several more thumbtacks, then stepped to the side. In neatly printed letters written with six different colored felt-tip markers, the poster said:

Dear Neighbors,

Hear ye! Hear ye! We join together in paying tribute to a great event. Poppin Road will soon have its very own newspaper. It will tell you everything you need to know about our neighbors and the world.

It will also give you plenty of advice. If you have problems (any kind) please write to "Dear Aunt Polly." She knows best. Just stick the letters in Glenda's mailbox.

Thank you for your cooperation.

Maisie Blumm & Glenda Jax, Publishers

"I can't read," said Brett, one of the four Larsen children.

"Me, neither," said his little brother, Eric, sitting on a tricycle.

Maisie cleared her throat the way Miss Lange sometimes did before she made an important announcement at school. "Boys and girls, if you're all very, very quiet, Miss Jax and I will read it to you."

"We're all boys," said Marshall.

"Be quiet anyway!" snapped Glenda. Then she and Maisie began reading their poster:

"Dear neighbors, Hear ye! Hear ye!" they chanted with such unusual sweetness in their voices that nobody in the crowd gathered around the telephone pole stirred. "We join together in paying . . ."

Robby, the littlest Larsen, stopped sucking his wet pretzel and let his hand drop to his side. Oxie sat next to him with his ears cocked. Marshall listened without blinking and the others breathed with their mouths open.

"Thank you all for your cooperation," Glenda said when she and Maisie finished. Then they each took a bow and blew kisses.

"Are there any questions?" asked Maisie.

"Who's Aunt Polly?" asked Marshall.

"The smartest woman in the world," said Glenda. "She's a lawyer."

"And a psychiatrist," said Maisie.

Glenda looked around, smiling. "Any other questions?"

"Who tooked my pwetzel?" asked little Robby Larsen.

His brother Brett pointed at Oxie. "Maisie's doggie did. He's eating it."

There was a piercing scream loud enough to send every mother on the block flying. Maisie quickly dug inside her pocket, looking for a piece of candy. "I don't have anything to shut him up," she said to Glenda. "Do you?"

Glenda ran her hands around the outside of her jeans. "Maybe," she said when she felt a lump. An old Life Saver was stuck to the lining of her pocket. She reached inside, peeled it off, and offered it to Robby. "You can have this if you stop screaming."

His scream stopped midthroat. "It's fuzzy," he said.

"Mmm. I know. That's what makes it yummy."

"Can we have some?" asked his brothers.

"Sorry, that's my last one," said Glenda. "But look . . . I'll tell you something special. There's going to be a secret about your family in our very first newspaper."

"What's your paper gonna say?" said Brett.

"That your mommy's having another baby."

"No, she's not."

"Yes, she is!"

Brett shook his head. "She didn't tell us."

"She didn't tell me, either," said Glenda. "But I saw her tummy. And that's how you know . . . by a big tummy."

"We already *have* a baby."

"So now you're getting another one!"

"And don't forget where you heard the news first, kids," Maisie said as they started back up the hill. "From Maisie and Glenda! Publishers of *The Poppin Road Gazette*."

•Chapter 4•

THE NEXT WEEK started off with a bang.

After recess Monday morning, Dr. Scotch got on the Fairview School intercom to tell the students they had received a telegram in care of Joseph Mandino, a third-grader.

"Joseph's right here in my office beside me," said Dr. Scotch, "and he would like to read his telegram. Joseph?"

There was a noise like an ocean's roar as Joseph breathed close to the mike. "Dear Joseph," he began, rather shakily. "Your blue balloon was found Saturday A.M. by our track team here at North Millbrook Girls Academy. Our school would like to wish yours a very happy birthday. Congratulations. Coach Joan Heggarty."

The telegram was the talk of the school—the first proof that a helium balloon could actually make it out of the town of Deer Creek. Whatever excitement had cooled off over the weekend, was stirred up again when students saw Joseph's tele-gram posted on the bulletin board outside the main office.

"How far away do you think North Millbrook is?" Glenda asked Maisie on the bus ride home from school.

"Thirty-five miles. Miss Lange showed us on the map."

Glenda pulled a notebook and pencil out of her book bag and started doing some arithmetic. "Let's see . . . if a balloon can travel thirty-five miles in one day, in three and a half days it could go . . ."

By the time they reached their stop on Poppin Road, they had figured out that one of their bal-loons could already be in New York, three and a half weeks away from Miami, and a little over two months away from Hollywood.

"That'd be in May," said Maisie. "About the time of the Deer Creek Dog Show."

"Hey, what's this? Dear Neighbors . . . Hear Ye! . . . Hear Ye!"

Maisie and Glenda glanced up, realizing for the first time that the bus had stopped.

"If you have problems . . . any kind . . . ha ha . . . please write to 'Dear Aunt Polly'!" Half the bus had crowded next to the windows on Bene-dict's side, listening to him read the poster tacked to the telephone pole. "Aunt Polly knows best!"

he said in a squeaky, squawky voice. "Caw, caw!"

Everyone around him doubled over, laughing.

"C'mon," said Maisie, zipping out of her seat. "Let's get out of here before he sees us."

She and Glenda ducked their heads down and did a running-crouch to the front of the bus. But not fast enough.

"Hey, Maisie-Daisy and Glender-Fender-Bender," Benedict shouted as they reached the steps. "Who's old Aunt Polly? Your parrot?"

Maisie and Glenda hopped off the bus, but Marshall, who was right behind them with Honey, didn't. "That's not funny, Benedict," he answered. "My Aunt Polly's the smartest person in the whole wide world. She's a lawyer and a scientist."

"And a doctor and a lion tamer!" Honey added. "So there!"

Maisie and Glenda ran lickety-split up the hill to Glenda's house without stopping till they got to the mailbox. Glenda collapsed on top of it, catching her breath. "I didn't think about the bus kids reading our poster, did you?"

Maisie shook her head. "I just thought we put it in the best place for people on our street to see it."

"Yeah, me too." Glenda opened her mailbox and took out the mail. "Maybe we should move the poster somewhere else," she said, leafing through the bills and catalogs. Then she shrieked. "It worked! We got one . . . a letter for 'Dear Aunt Polly'!"

"Who's it from?" asked Maisie.

Glenda turned the envelope over. "Doesn't say. C'mon. Let's open it in my room."

Mrs. Jax was standing in the hallway, waiting to greet them, but they whizzed right by her and went upstairs. "Don't I even get a hello?" she called.

"Hello," they called back and kept on going.

The shades were down and Glenda's room was dark and smelled a little like stale toast. She turned on the light. Her top bunk, with its pink-striped bedspread, was made up as neat as a package. But the bottom bunk was nearly as rumpled as Lloyd's bed. She and Maisie plopped their books next to a pile of stuffed animals and sat in the middle.

"Hurry . . . see what it says," said Maisie.

Glenda slid her fingers under the glued flap and ripped open the envelope.

Dear Aunt Polly,

Maybe you can help me with my problem. I had a baby six months ago and I guess I still look fat. Yesterday, my oldest son told me a newspaper was going to announce that I was expecting again. But I'm not.

Can you suggest a diet? I'd appreciate your help.

Yours truly,
Not Currently Pregnant

"Shoot!" said Glenda. "There goes our news about Mrs. Larsen. What'll we do? Put her on a diet?"

"We have to. It's our responsibility," said Maisie. "Only I don't know any good ones. Do you?"

"My mom's been on about fifty."

"So's mine. But she never loses weight."

"Why? She cheats?"

Maisie nodded. "Yeah, sure. Especially when she's on that cottage cheese and grapefruit thing. She'll wait till we're all in bed, then get up and eat a pie. Lloyd's caught her."

"Betcha I know where she got that diet," Glenda said, as she crossed the room to raise her shades. "From my mom. Think about it. If someone wants to lose weight, who do they call? Some other chubbette who's dieting. Nobody's ever smart enough to ask a skinny kid how to eat."

"Mrs. Larsen did. She wrote to us."

"Aha! That's the point, Maisie. She wrote to Aunt Polly. Probably thinks she's another roly-poly diet expert." Glenda came back and sat down.

"Look at us. Bones, bones, and more bones. We're the *real* experts. We should make up the diet."

"How? By keeping track of what we eat?"

"Right. If we each did it for a week, we could put together a two-week menu . . . call it 'Aunt Polly's Fourteen-Day Wonder.' "

"But we don't have time. We want our newspaper out next weekend."

"Hmm." Glenda cupped her chin in her hands. "Who else besides us weighs under eighty?"

"Marshall and Honey."

"Well, there you go. The four of us will make up Mrs. Larsen's diet."

HONEY was a snap to convince. After dinner Maisie simply gave her an old used spiral notebook with a few good pages left and told her to make a list of everything she ate for three and a half days, starting with that morning.

Marshall, on the other hand, refused to co-operate.

"Did he say why?" Maisie asked Glenda, when they spoke on the phone before going to bed.

"He said it was none of the newspaper's business what he ate."

"But we won't print his name."

"I told him that," said Glenda. "I even told him

it was okay to write the list for two days. I thought we could make the diet an eight-day wonder. But he still won't help."

"Would a bribe work?"

"I tried a dime. That's all I have."

"Make him some kind of promise," said Maisie. "Say we'll tell him a deep, dark secret. Or take him someplace special."

When she got in bed, she had a vague feeling that something was wrong with the newspaper and couldn't sleep. The feeling had started while she and Glenda were on the phone. Something one or the other of them had said—was it a word?—had reminded her at the time that they were overlooking a big, important aspect of the newspaper business.

Then they'd kept talking about Marshall and she'd forgotten.

The feeling went from vague to terrible when she turned on her mini-light and tried reading her new book. Staring at the pages seemed to do it. She closed her book, clicked off the light, and stared up at the dark ceiling.

Then it hit her. *Print!* How were they going to *print* their newspaper?

On went her big light, her blue terry cloth robe, and her furry bear slippers. She padded downstairs and through the dark hall to the back of the house. The door to the den was closed. Lying on his back in front of it, all relaxed and stretched out like a sunbather, was Oxie. He was snoring. Maisie stepped over him and turned the knob. Her parents were inside, watching the *Ten O'Clock News*. She knew they were going to be mad as blazes seeing her up this late, but it didn't matter. She had to talk to them.

"*Now* what's going on upstairs?" her dad said when she came in. "Is Lloyd still playing his stereo?"

Mrs. Blumm sighed. "I told Honey to tell him to turn it off the last time *she* was down here."

Maisie snuggled in between them on the couch and laid her head on her mother's shoulder. "It's something else," she said. "I've got a terrible problem."

Both her parents turned to her, looking concerned. "Aw, Maze," her mother said, her voice all soft and buttery. "You're not worried about your height again, are you?"

Maisie shook her head.

"Is it your math?" asked her dad.

She bit her lip and looked up at him. "You know how hard Glenda and I've been working on our newspaper? Well, it's almost done, but now we can't . . ."

"Can't what?" asked her dad. "Tell us, sweetheart."

Maisie burst out crying. ". . . can't *print* it. We don't have a printing press!"

Her dad got up and turned off the TV set and her mom put her arm around her. "There are other ways of printing papers," she said.

"Yeah, I know . . . with a computer!" Maisie said, wiping her nose with an old tissue she found in the pocket of her robe. "But we don't have one. And neither does Glenda."

"There's always the copying machine at the library," her dad said. "How many pages do you have?"

"Six so far. But we'll have more. Ten, maybe."

"And you want to give every family on the street a free copy?"

Now Mrs. Blumm looked worried. "Sixteen families times ten pages is a hundred sixty pages, Ted," she said to Mr. Blumm. "At ten cents a page, it'd cost sixteen dollars to have them copied."

Mr. Blumm sank back on the couch. "That's a *lot* of money."

They were all quiet for a spell, except for Maisie's sniffling. Finally, Mrs. Blumm said, "Know what I think? We should all get a good night's sleep. Maybe one of us will wake up with a solution."

MAISIE didn't. She tossed and turned most of the night, thinking the newspaper was hopeless. She and Glenda didn't have many choices. Two, actually. They could make sixteen hand-written copies of the paper, or they could sell it for a dollar a copy. But then, of course, nobody would buy it. Even the Sunday edition of *The Deer Creek Chronicle* didn't cost that much.

Clothes were the last thing on her mind when she got up. She pulled out the first shirt and pair of jeans she found in her drawers and stuck them on. Then she thumped downstairs to the kitchen, feeling crankier than a grizzly bear.

The music on the radio didn't help. WKPR was playing "Mega-Love," its top hit of the week, and Lloyd, frying eggs, was tapping out the rhythm with a spatula on the edge of the stove.

Maisie wanted to throw the radio in the garbage. Instead she asked, "Where's Mom?"

Lloyd didn't answer. Neither did Honey. She was busy pouring breakfast cereal into a measuring cup. "One third cup of Oat Frooties and two tablespoons of sugar," she said, as she wrote in Maisie's old spiral notebook.

"Where's Mom?"

Honey dribbled a tiny bit of milk on her Oat Frooties, just enough to moisten them, and looked up at Maisie. "It's Tuesday. Remember?"

Darn! Maisie had forgotten. It *was* Tuesday—the day their mom went to the hardware store with their dad to do the bookkeeping. "Did she leave already?"

Honey took a bite out of something red. "A piece of toast with no crust and gobs and gobs of jam," she said, writing in the notebook.

"I said, did she leave already?"

Honey kept writing and Lloyd turned off the stove and carried his plate to the table, singing, "Oh, oh, ohh, my-ah mega-love . . . won't you bee-ah my-ah mega-love?"

Maisie kicked a table leg. *"Would somebody give me an answer?"*

Lloyd sprinkled pepper on his five fried eggs. "Like what's the matter with you?"

"I want to know if Mom's left."

"Like a while ago. You were still sleeping."

Honey licked jam off the corner of her mouth. "She left you a note by the toaster. It's got a little butter on it."

Maisie went over to the counter and picked up the note. "Not a little butter. A lot!" she said, wiping it off with a napkin.

"Like, hey! You ever stop complaining?" Lloyd asked.

Maisie ignored him and read the note. Her mother apologized for not waking her up to talk to her before she left, but added, *You were sleeping so soundly, I didn't have the heart to.*

If you and Glenda want to run the following ad in your paper, Daddy and I will pay you twenty-five cents a line.

DEER CREEK PAINT & HARDWARE CO., INC.

*Hardware Supplies   *Power Tools
*Paints & Varnishes   *Garden Shop
*Storm Windows & Doors

Headquarters for Do-It-Yourselfers
Mary & Ted Blumm, owners

Maisie counted the lines as she split open an English muffin with a fork. There were . . .

"Better hurry. The bus is coming in ten minutes," said Honey.

Six. And at a quarter a line, that would give her and Glenda . . .

"And like it's your turn to get Oxie in the house," Lloyd said, putting his plate in the dishwasher.

Wow! A dollar fifty. This *was* the solution—taking money for ads.

MAISIE ran to the bus stop eating her English muffin. Everybody else on the street was already on the bus. But the driver was waiting for her.

So was Oxie. Shoot! She'd forgotten to get him in the house.

"Come!" she commanded.

Oxie perked one ear when he heard her and took off.

Maisie watched him tear across the street to the Rigbys' yard. "Come back and I'll give you a cookie," she hollered, holding up what was left of her muffin. But that didn't stop Oxie. He ran from the Rigbys' yard to the Larsens' to the Whittakers'.

Maisie gave up and climbed the steps into the bus. Dumb dog! She'd have to leave him outside till she came home from school.

"Better go back and get him quick," said the driver. "Look who's coming."

Maisie gasped. A familiar white van was heading up Poppin Road—*Rosemary Hall, the Deer Creek dogcatcher*! Maisie hopped off the bus and ran down the street. The van had already pulled up to the curb in front of the Whittakers'. Out climbed Rosemary, a moon-faced woman with short blond hair and a big rear end that filled her blue uniform pants like two overgrown pumpkins. Oxie sat on the grass, watching her with interest. She walked to the back of the van, opened the door, and leaned against it. Oxie seemed to recognize her from the last time she caught him. He got up, wagging his tail, and trotted toward her.

"Don't do it, Oxie!" Maisie screamed.

"Don't do it, Oxie!" screamed what sounded like an army behind her.

Maisie glanced back. Everybody on the bus had gotten off to help. Glenda, the three Rigby girls, and most of the kids from Barnes Lane were swarming the Larsens' yard. Across the street, Honey and Marshall were leading a band of sixth-graders around the hedges between the Klines' driveway and the Hewitts'.

"Come on back here, sweetie boy," called Honey.

Oxie was so excited by the commotion he was causing, he danced in one direction with his tongue out and his big, bushy tail churning the air, then turned and danced in the other. He couldn't decide who to go to.

As Maisie stood in the Larsens' driveway, pleading with him to come to her, she saw Benedict dart out from behind some bushes a few feet away. He stopped a second, removed his sandwich from his lunch bag, then crept onto the Whittakers' lawn.

The dogcatcher also saw him and slapped her thigh to get Oxie's attention.

Oxie stopped dancing around, looked at Rosemary, perked his ears, and listened to the dogs she'd already caught, yowling and howling in the van. Then he looked at Benedict. Benedict tore off a piece of his sandwich and dropped it on the grass. Then he tore off another piece and another. Oxie sniffed the ground. Benedict had left a trail of white bread and red meat that led up to a bed of crocuses by the side of the Whittakers' porch. Oxie snatched the first piece, ate it, wagged his tail, and went on to the next.

Maisie stayed in the driveway, holding her breath. She'd tried Benedict's trick herself, using a hot dog. Darn! She knew what was going to happen. As soon as Oxie got that last piece of meat and Benedict made a grab for him, he'd streak off again.

Rosemary gave her thigh another slap. But Oxie had lost interest. Something new had aroused his curiosity—a body on the ground. It was Benedict, lying flat as a board next to the bed of crocuses. What is he doing? Maisie wondered. He looked as if he'd been knocked out cold.

Oxie was equally puzzled. He sniffed Benedict's sneakers, his socks and jeans, working his way up to Benedict's denim jacket. Benedict showed no signs of life. Oxie nudged him with his nose. Still nothing. He pawed the ground, whimpering, then began licking Benedict's face. Slowly, Bendict reached up and slipped his fingers under Oxie's collar. He had him!

"Atta good boy," he said, sitting up. Then he called over to Rosemary, "Did you see that? This husky's specially trained to rescue children! You ought to leave him alone!"

The dogcatcher got in her van, slammed the door, and pulled away to a loud round of applause up and down the street.

"Okay, Screwy . . . let's go to your mother," Benedict said, running Oxie over to Maisie, who, in turn, ran him up the hill as if they were part of a relay team. Halfway up, Honey dashed out of the Hewitts' driveway.

They both took Oxie into their house, and when they came outside, everybody was back on the bus. The engine was running. "Okay, gang . . . let's make tracks," said the driver. "We're six minutes behind schedule."

Honey slid into the seat next to Marshall, and Maisie headed down the aisle to sit with Glenda. As she passed Benedict, she stopped to thank him. "That was really a smart trick," she said.

Benedict shrugged. His lap was filled with cookies, apples, oranges, little bags of carrot sticks, candy, and sandwiches. A collection had been made to replace his lunch. "It's like this," he said, chomping into an oozing jelly donut, "when you're dealing with intelligent, highly trained animals, you gotta stay cool."

Maisie knew he was kidding and smiled. "I wish I had something to give you for lunch, but I buy mine."

"Aw, you poor kid. No wonder you look under-fed. Here. Have something nutritious," he said, handing her a chocolate bar and a package of Twinkies.

Maisie shared them with Glenda as the bus headed along Hardknob Drive. "Don't forget," Glenda said, licking melted chocolate off her fingers, "we have to write this down. As an after-breakfast snack for Mrs. Larsen's diet."

"Did you ever talk Marshall into writing down what he eats?" asked Maisie.

Glenda nodded. "Sure. But it took a while. And he'll only do it for one day. I promised we'd show him a pigsty."

"Where? On a farm?"

"Uh-uh. In your house. We'll take him to Lloyd's room."

They were turning into the school driveway and Maisie suddenly remembered the note her mother had left next to the toaster. "Here. Quick . . . look at this ad," she said, pulling the note out of her pocket to show Glenda. "My mom and dad'll pay us a dollar fifty if we run it in our newspaper."

"*A dollar fifty!*" Glenda's eyes bugged. "Hey!

Ads. What a great idea! Just think. If we got them from everybody in the neighborhood . . ."

The bus had pulled up in front of the school and the bus driver was telling everybody to hustle. They had one minute before the bell rang.

As Maisie and Glenda hurried up the walk to the entrance, Glenda's mind was working like a cash register. "I mean, even if we got ads from only *half* the neighborhood, we'd be rich. Really *rolling* in money."

"Uh-uh. The money's going to have to go for the newspaper. To pay the library," said Maisie.

"The *library*!" roared Glenda. "You crazy? Not *my* money!"

"Oh, yeah? What're you planning to do? Write out all sixteen copies yourself? By *hand*?"

"I'm not writing out sixteen copies of anything by hand!"

Maisie bristled as she reached for the door. "Oh, I see! *I'm* supposed to do all the hard stuff. And *you're* supposed to keep all the money!"

"I never said—"

Bbbrrring! went the bell.

Glenda stomped off toward Mr. Bingham's classroom and Maisie stomped off toward Miss Lange's. For most of the day, it looked as if *The Poppin Road Gazette* was a lost cause. The publishers didn't play with each other during recess, speak, or eat lunch together at noon. They rode in silence, two seats apart, coming home from school on the bus, then walked up the hill separately.

But the mail in Glenda's mailbox changed things.

No sooner had Maisie gone home by herself, and started making brownies, than the phone rang. Glenda was calling. "Maisie, you won't believe this! Guess what? We got three more letters for 'Dear Aunt Polly.' "

Maisie turned on the oven. "Too bad we can't use them."

"Of course we can. I'll come over now," said Glenda, "so we can think up answers."

"It won't do us any good. You don't want to pay for the copying machine at the library."

Glenda groaned. "What's wrong with using my *dad's* copying machine?"

"He has one?"

"Sure, he does . . . at his office. And it's *free*! He'll let us run off as many copies as we want."

"Well, why didn't you tell me?"

"I tried, but—"

"Never mind," said Maisie. "Just get over here quick. I'm making brownies."

When she hung up, she couldn't stop smiling. How about that! Their newspaper wouldn't cost a cent. Maybe they would be rolling in money.

·Chapter 5·

SATURDAY afternoon, Maisie and Glenda rode downtown with Mr. Jax, carrying a large manila envelope that contained the first edition of *The Poppin Road Gazette*. Both girls were completely satisfied with their efforts. They'd answered all the letters to Dear Aunt Polly, shortened Mrs. Larsen's diet, but in such a way that it *appeared* to be longer, and they'd painstakingly written out every page they wanted copied . . . well, almost every page, in their finest penmanship.

After Mr. Jax showed them how to operate his copying machine, Glenda placed the front page face down under the machine's lid, pressed the button, and cried, "Let it roll!"

Maisie stood beside her, clasping her hands. "A newspaper is born," she whispered, feeling all choked up inside as they watched the first copy of the front page slide into the tray.

Copies were made for every family on Poppin

Road, plus two extras—one for each girl to save for her grandchildren. Then at six o'clock sharp, the next morning, Maisie and Glenda left a paper on the doorstep of every house in their neighborhood.

They'd purposely planned it that way, so they could beat the boy who delivered *The Deer Creek Chronicle*.

HE

POPPIN ROAD GAZETTE

1st Edition

Maisie Blumm and Glenda Jax, Publishers

Lady Di's Outfit

Quail. It sort of looks like chicken.

KRA→

←Rice

←Shrimp

The White House Dinner

WORLD NEWS

Lady Di did it again. She was in Scotland this week visiting hospitals. She had on a blue hat with a veil and a feather. Her dress wasn't so great though. It sort of looked like a bathrobe with a frilly lace collar.

Charles and the kids stayed home doing nothing in their castle.

×× ——————— ××

U.S. News

The White House had a big party Saturday. The president wanted to thank Country Folk singers for doing a good job! But the food was pretty gross. Ugh. They had to eat shrimp and quail and cooked OKRA! Johnny Cash wore his same old black shirt and pants again.

* * * * * * * * *

Unscramble these words: Pppnio doaR Getzate

Answer:

Poppin Road Gazette

Everybody should know what's going on in their neighborhood. Read this column to find out what's happening in ours.

Did You Know ??

— Bonnie Rigby has a massive crush on a high school football player? We don't know his name yet, but his number is 47.

— The Rosens are moving to New Jersey. They're so nice we'll all miss them, _sob sob_! But we want another nice family to buy their house. So nobody tell that their basement floods when it rains, okay?

— Alice Jax doesn't have gray and brown hair anymore. She washed out all that dull gray with Clairol.

— A big miracle happened at the Blumm's. Lloyd finally cleaned his room. But in our opinion he didn't do a very good job. ☹

— Mr. Hewitt ran a 6 mile race last week. He won a medal for 3rd place in his age group (30-40 years). We think it's terrific that someone that old can still run. ~~YAY~~ for you, Mr. H. ! ☺

— Mrs. Kline will be collecting for the HEART FUND this month. Try not to give her bad checks. REMEMBER: HEARTS ARE IMPORTANT to HEALTH !! ♥

Up, Up and Away...

The story you've been DYING to read!

March 16 was VERY exciting. Fairview School celebrated its 10th birthday. The P.T.A. baked a giant cake and bought 572 balloons. Then a bunch of people with machines came to school and filled the balloons with helium.

Every kid got a balloon and wrote a letter to tie to it.

WHERE WILL THOSE BALLOONS GO?
China? Hollywood? South Pole?

Everyone sang HAPPY 10th BIRTHDAY before the sendoff out on the baseball field. Only one person didn't listen. We won't say who he was. But you know him.

* * * * * * *

VERY IMPORTANT ANNOUNCEMENT:

In may, two of our neighborhood's most beautiful pets will be in THE DEER CREEK DOG SHOW.
THEIR PICTURES

MY DOG SNODKUMS
SITTING. BY Glenda J.

MY DOG OXIE PLAYING
DEAD. BY MAISIE B.

a Riddle
Why did the elephant wear purple sneakers? Answer: His white ones were in the wash.

a maze

↑ START

SPRING IS HERE! ☺

Aunt Polly

THIS is THE FAMOUS Aunt Polly!

She knows everything.
- Is your lovelife rotten?
- Are there stains on your carpet?

Just write and ask Aunt Polly what to do. She'll give you advice like nobody else can!

* * *

This week's letters and answers

Dear Aunt Polly,

Maybe you can help me with my problem. I had a baby 6 months ago and I guess I still look fat. Yesterday my oldest son told me a newspaper was going to announce that I was expecting again. But I'm not. Can you suggest a diet? I'd appreciate your help.

Yours truly,
not Currently Pregnant

Dear Not Currently P.G.,

Stop worrying and get with it. You need exercise. Run up and down the street 86 times a week and follow my special diet.

You must eat everything!

AUNT POLLY'S 28 DAY WONDER DIET. STAMP OUT FAT!

First Day

Breakfast - ⅓ Cup Oat Frooties, 2 T. sugar, 1 t. milk, Toast with no crust, but gobs of jam.

Snack - 2 Twinkies, 1 fireball jawbreaker.

Lunch - Box of cherry cough drops and water.

Dinner - 2 bites meatloaf, 3 bites salad, mashed potatoes, all the mint-chip ice cream you want.

Bedtime - Rootbeer and vanilla cupcake

* * *

REMEMBER: EAT RIGHT, GET SKINNY!

Second Day

Breakfast – 1 corn muffin, handful of Oat Frooties while you get dressed.

Snack – ½ box Cracker Jacks, bag of gummy bears.

Lunch – 2 bites Tunafish chow mane and more gummy bears.

3 P.m. – a Shirley Temple, 3 squares marshmallow Krispies

Dinner – BBQ'd chicken (or quail) corn on cob, Buttered noodles

Bedtime – 1 ½ brownies and water

* * * * *

Third Day

Breakfast – 2 frozen waffles with syrup, 7-up

Snack – candy bar and donut

Lunch – Fairview School pizza, ½ carton milk

3 P.m. – Popcorn and butterscotch crunch (pick out the nuts.)

Dinner – Chicken pot pie (pick out the peas), Biskit, 5 green beans, 12 olives

Bedtime – Popcorn and bubble gum

* * * * *

Fourth Day

Breakfast – Peanut butter sandwich, Strawberry Quik

Lunch – Go to Burger-hutch
① Hutchburger ③ Fries, ③ shake
④ apple pie

Snack – Grapes, Oat Frooties, ½ apple (no skin), donut

Dinner – Pot roast with A-1 sauce and ketchup, Potato, 1 slice zucchini

Bedtime – water and another donut

* * * * *

Repeat this diet 7 times. Soon you'll weigh about 65 pounds. Love, Aunt Polly

MORE letters to FAMOUS Aunt Polly...

Dear Aunt Polly,
I'm mad. I loaned this kid on our street my new KRAZY-KAT game and now he won't give it back. How can I get it?

Love,
Mad

*   *   *

Dear Mad,
Use your head! Borrow the kid's bike and keep it till he brings back your game. If that doe (oops) doesn't work, beat him up!

Love,
Aunt Polly

*   *   *   *

Dear Aunt Polly,
My son is wonderful but we argue about his messy room. I get a headache when I see it. I've taken away his allowance, but it hasn't worked. Do you have any ideas?

Love,
a Fed-Up Mom

*   *   *

Dear Fed-Up,
Just be glad your son isn't a burglar or a hijacker. Shut his door and stay out of his room. Headaches will make you mean to the rest of your family. Think of them!

Love,
Aunt Polly

*   *   *   *

Watching-Birdie

Watching-Birdie is Watching YOU! Is your yard as pretty as the Whittakers? Do you have a billion CROCUSES? NO? Well, why not? Seeing CROCUSES makes people feel good.

Be a good neighbor. Copy the WHittakers. TODAY!
Plant crocuses!

Dear Aunt Polly,

I get so worn out I need a half hour nap in the afternoon. But my children won't let me. They bother me and wake me up.

How can I get some rest?

Love,
Tired Mother

Dear Tired Mother,

You're a grown-up, aren't you? Grown-ups don't <u>need</u> naps.

Do fun things with your kids. Make them gingerbread houses or play touch football with them. Take them to a <u>circus</u>!

That will make you peppy again.

Love,
Aunt Polly

🙂 * * *

KEEP YOUR LETTERS COMING IN, FOLKS!

* * * *

Riddle #2: Why did the little nerd keep the door open when he took his bath?

ANSWER: So nobody could PEEK at him through the keyhole. HA! HA!

♥ ♥ ♥ ♥

Knock, KNOCK!!

Guess <u>who's</u> coming to SEE you next week? That's right... the publishers of this newspaper. Maisie and Glenda.

We'll be around to take ads and see what you think of <u>THE POPPIN ROAD GAZETTE</u>.

Do you have a suggestion?
A favorite column?
A news item?
A <u>BIG</u> ad?

* * * * * * *

#1. JOKE of the WEEK

A guy goes into a pet shop. "Hey, I like that parrot," he says to the owner. "But why's he got strings tied on his legs?"

"Ya pull his right string and he sings Yankee Doodle," says the pet store owner. (oops) "Ya pull his left string and he whistles Dixie."

"Oh yeah? Well, what'd happen if I pulled both strings at the same time?" says the guy.

"You'd knock me flat on my rump!" screams the parrot.

•Chapter 6•

AH, SPRING vacation!

Maisie and Glenda had wonderful plans for the next nine days. They were going to train Oxie and Snookums for the Deer Creek Dog Show, dye Easter eggs, and sunbathe if it ever stopped raining.

But business was business. First they had to get out the second edition of *The Poppin Road Gazette*. The first one hadn't made them rich exactly (they earned $7.25 in ads), but it had been a hit. Nearly a dozen letters poured in from readers who liked the advice from "Dear Aunt Polly." One, signed by *Someone Who Hates Counting Calories*, said it made his day to learn he could eat Oat Frooties for breakfast.

Maisie and Glenda figured Mr. Jax wrote it. He'd gone out and bought a giant, economy-size box.

As for another letter saying, *Thank you for telling*

me to stay out of my son's room . . . it's going to be a pleasure not to argue with him about cleaning it anymore, they knew for certain who it was from. Maisie's mother.

Mrs. Blumm decided she had nothing to lose by trying a new tactic. Taking away Lloyd's allowance hadn't worked. So if he wanted his room to look like a junkyard, that was his business, not hers, she told her family one night. All she asked was that he keep his door shut so she never had to see it.

About that, Lloyd was thrilled.

And Maisie and <u>Glenda</u> were walking on air over the reaction to their paper. By going from door to door, selling ads for the coming edition, they learned that seven of the sixteen families living on their street had enjoyed the "Did You Know?" column best, and the nine other families favored "Dear Aunt Polly."

We aim to please our neighbors, became their newspaper's motto.

From then on, jokes, riddles, and world and national news would be cut to a half-page or less. The rest of the paper would be devoted, exclusively, to ads and the two favorite columns. And there was another change.

The newspaper was going to be typed.

Mrs. Jax was letting the two girls use her portable typewriter, and they'd set up an office for themselves in the corner of the Jaxes' basement storage room.

THE HOME OF *THE POPPIN ROAD GAZETTE*

G. Jax and M. Blumm, Publishers

said the sign on the door.

Their desk was an old redwood picnic table. Both of them could sit on the picnic bench and work at their desk together. To organize themselves, they were using an empty soup can for pencils, a cigar box for ad money, a shoe box for unanswered letters to Aunt Polly, another shoe box for answered letters, a sweater box labeled MISC. for anything that didn't go in the shoe boxes, and a kitchen tray for pages that were typed and ready to be run off on the copier.

Their typing wasn't fancy. They used what Mrs. Jax called the "hunt and peck method." When each girl took her turn, she would hunt all over the keys for the letter she wanted, then peck at it with one finger. It was taking lots of time, but the finished pages were turning out much neater than when they'd been handwritten.

"So now we won't have any complaints that the paper's hard to read," Maisie said, as she searched the keys for P.

"Over there," Glenda said, pointing to the right. "The last letter in the second row."

Actually, there had been only one complaint. From Lloyd. He'd been mad when he saw his name and read about his room in the "Did You Know?" column.

"Hey! Like what's this mean . . . *Hoyd* finally *deaned* his room?" he shouted at Maisie.

"*Lloyd*, not *Hoyd*!" she said. "*Lloyd* finally *cl*eaned his room. That's a *cl*, not a *d*!"

Lloyd was still mad. And he told Maisie if she or Glenda ever so much as set a little toe inside his room again, they were goners. "Like you'll be known as the *late* publishers of *The Poppin Road Gazette*!"

Since then he'd locked the door to his room whenever he was in there, and he said he'd set up booby traps to catch them when he wasn't. Maisie didn't know what the booby traps were, but she believed him. There were warning signs on his door. And he'd attached something so he could tell if it was opened.

"Oh, he's just fooling you," Glenda said, when Maisie told her the story while they were working in their office.

"Nope. He really does have something. I tested it," said Maisie. "All I did was go in there for a second, yesterday, and when he came home he knew."

Glenda tallied up the new ads for the paper. They had eight, so far. "Well, we've got to figure out some way of getting inside."

"Because of the promise you made Marshall?"

"Yeah. I thought maybe he'd forget. But he keeps nagging me."

Maisie erased the X she'd typed by mistake. "Too bad we can't take him to a real farm."

"Naw. Knowing Marshall, he'd rather see how Lloyd lives than how a pig lives."

♦ ♦ ♦

BY THE middle of the week, the second edition of *The Poppin Road Gazette* was finished except for answering one last letter to "Dear Aunt Polly." Maisie found the letter in the Jaxes' mailbox when she was crossing the street to see Glenda, Wednesday morning. They'd planned to sunbathe, but it was raining again.

Glenda sat on the picnic bench in front of the typewriter and slid in a fresh sheet of typing paper. "Okay. Read the letter to me."

"Dear Aunt Polly," Maisie read from a sheet of pink paper,

"I'm in junior high and there's this really CUTE ♠ boy who rides my bus. (You know the type.) I give him candy and gum, even my seat sometimes. Once I made him saltwater taffy because I heard him say he liked it. But he never thanked me. He doesn't even notice me. How can I get his attention?"

"Truly Lovesick."

"Hmmm." Glenda sank her chin in her hands, thinking. The first thing she and Maisie did when they got a letter was try to figure out who sent it. Next they decided if it was a joke.

"It's gotta be from Wendy Whittaker," said Maisie. "And it's not a joke. Look at the hearts she drew around cute."

Glenda sat up tall and held her hands high above the typewriter like a concert pianist. Then she went to town typing out the letter. When she finished, she started a new paragraph. "Dear Truly Lovesick," it began.

"Now what?" she said to Maisie.

"Beats me. I've never been lovesick."

"Me either," said Glenda, "but I sure know what I'd do if some jerk didn't thank me for making him saltwater taffy. That stuff takes forever to make. And it sticks to everything in the kitchen."

"You want to write the advice yourself?"

"Yeah. Could I?"

While Maisie fiddled with the tray, restacking the papers that were ready to be copied, Glenda typed. She seemed to be getting pretty good at it. Right now, she was typing with two fingers. And from the way her jaw was set, Maisie knew that Wendy Whittaker was getting excellent advice on how to handle her love life.

"All done," said Glenda. She whipped the paper out of the typewriter and handed it to Maisie. "What do you think?"

Dear Truly Lovesick,
   If you want that cute boy's attention, stop giving him things! Take *his* candy and gum. Grab *his* seat. Try tripping him when he gets off the bus. And don't make any more saltwater taffy until you're engaged!

Love,
Aunt Polly

Maisie thought the advice was perfect. "He'll probably get a crush on Wendy in two days," she said, putting the paper on the tray. "Well, we're done. What do you want to do? Train dogs or dye Easter eggs?"

"Both."

They got a carton of eggs out of the Jaxes' refrigerator and an umbrella from the hall closet and headed across the street to Maisie's house, carrying Snookums.

While their eggs boiled in a big pot, Maisie lured Oxie into the den with a liver-flavored dog biscuit. Glenda and Snookums were already in there, waiting. It was time to begin serious training for the dog show.

"Off!" Maisie said as Oxie hopped onto the couch. "You're not supposed to be on there. Now get off!"

Oxie paid no attention to her and curled up in his favorite spot, gnawing his biscuit.

"Don't forget! You're in dog training school!" she scolded.

He didn't care.

She sighed and turned to Glenda. "It's the rain . . . it makes him lazy," she explained. "Why don't you and Snookums go first? And I'll judge."

Glenda carried four-pound Snookums to the middle of the room. "Okay, sweetie," she said, patting the little tuft of hair that was clamped upright with a barrette on top of Snookums' head. "Pretend this is a real dog show. See? There's Maisie, the judge. And over there," she said, twisting Snookums's head toward Oxie, "is the other doggie you'll be competing against."

She stooped down as if she were placing a fragile glass doll on the floor. "There you go, sweetie. Now when I tell you to sit, I want you to sit. Okay? Now on your mark, get ready . . . *sit*!"

Snookums stood as rigid as a footstool between Glenda's feet.

"No, no. You've got to *bend* your legs to sit."
Glenda stooped down and pushed Snookums' tiny,
rigid rump onto the floor. "That's better. Now
you're sitting," she said. But as soon as she re-
leased her hand, Snookums' tiny rump popped
up again.

Glenda glanced over at Maisie. "I guess Snookums doesn't like to sit in strange houses."

Both girls were relieved when the timer buzzed
in the kitchen, telling them their eggs had boiled
ten minutes. Oxie beat them out there and stood
howling in front of the stove until Maisie shut off
the timer. "Good boy! You knew our eggs were
done, didn't you?" she said, patting his head.

Glenda looked doubtful. "He did?"

"Oh, sure. He never lets us overcook anything.
Roasts, noodles, fried chicken . . ." Maisie lifted
the pot off the burner and poured the boiling
water in the sink ". . . turkeys, cakes. He always
tells us when they're ready."

While she lined up six teacups on the counter
and dissolved a dye pellet with vinegar and water
in each of them, Glenda set Snookums on the
floor. "Stand, Snookums!" she ordered. Then she
squealed, *"Whatta good girl!"*

"Want to do anything while our eggs cool?"
asked Maisie.

"That depends. Who's home?"

"Nobody. Mom's doing inventory at the store and Honey's at your house."

"Where's Lloyd?"

"Downtown buying records."

Glenda started tiptoeing out of the kitchen. "Come on," she whispered. "Now's our chance to see if his room's really booby-trapped."

Oxie seemed to know just what the girls were up to. With a wild, shiny look in his eyes, he raced upstairs ahead of them. Right behind him was Snookums. When Maisie and Glenda got to Lloyd's room, both dogs were sitting in front of the door.

"Good boy, Oxie!" said Maisie.

"Good girl, Snookums!" said Glenda. Then, without wasting a minute, she got down on her knees and put her head on the floor, trying to peer into Lloyd's room through the crack under his door.

"See anything?" asked Maisie.

"The edge of his rug."

"Let me look." Maisie knelt down between Glenda and Oxie.

"The dogs smell something," Glenda whispered.

"How do you know?"

"Watch them. They keep sniffing along the crack."

Maisie watched a second, then slid close enough

to the crack to stick her nose in it. There was a slightly unpleasant, musty odor coming from Lloyd's room, but nothing unexpected. She sniffed, then sniffed again, taking a deep whiff, and just as she did, she felt something fuzzy go up one nostril. "Eww, yuckkk!" she screamed, sitting back on her heels.

"What was it? What'd you smell?" asked Glenda.

"A spider!" Maisie shrieked, clawing at her nose. "It must be a spider!"

Glenda shot away from the crack. "I didn't know they smelled."

"No, no! In my nose! It crawled in my nose!"

"Then blow . . . get it out quick! Before it lays eggs in your head."

Maisie was in such a panic, she rolled on the floor, hammering it with her fists and making such strange noises, blowing and snorting, that both dogs cowered behind Glenda. "Did anything come out?" she asked.

"*Eww!*" Glenda leaned forward, looking at the gray, woolly thing at the end of her nostril. "It's a dustball."

Maisie picked it off her nose and rubbed it between her fingers to make sure it wasn't alive. She'd had enough sniffing around Lloyd's door.

So had Glenda. "Let's just go in there," she said, reaching for the knob.

"Be careful. Lloyd's probably rigged up bricks to fall on our heads."

Glenda pushed the door open about an inch, waited for a crash, then when there wasn't one, pushed the door open a little wider. "Safe so far."

"You still shouldn't let Snookums in there."

"*Snookums, don't!*"

It was too late. Snookums had already squeezed through the narrow opening and hopped into the room. Maisie and Glenda clamped their hands over their mouths, afraid of what might happen to her.

"She seems okay . . . she's not yelping," Glenda said after a minute.

"But why'd she hop like that?"

"Hop like what?"

"When she went in there. Didn't you see? She acted like something was on the floor."

Both girls crawled up close to the door to see what it was. "There . . . about two inches off the floor," said Maisie. "Lloyd's strung blue thread across his door to trip us!"

"Nobody's that stupid."

"Then why's it there?"

"Must be for something else," said Glenda. "If he'd really wanted to trip us, he would've used rope."

She was feeling along the bottom edge of the door and Maisie was watching.

"What're you doing?"

"Trying to see where the thread's coming from. Ah! Here we go . . . where my finger is."

"You feel it?"

Glenda nodded. "Yep. He's taped one end of it under here. See?" she said, pulling out a piece of thread about three inches long. "This is what's hanging down."

Before either of them had a chance to reach around the door to feel where the other end of the thread was taped, Oxie lunged against the door, flinging it wide open.

"Darn you, Oxie!" Maisie yelled when she saw the thread lying on the floor. "You popped it off! Now we'll never see where it went."

"No, wait. Look!" Glenda had poked her head inside the room. "It's right here . . . taped to his dustboard. The other end popped off. The one taped to the bottom of the door. Hey, I'll bet . . ."

Suddenly she crawled all the way into the room and shut the door, leaving Maisie alone in the hall. "I'm sliding the thread under," she called. "Tell me when you've taped it back to the bottom of the door."

"Okay. It's back. Now what?"

"Bang the door open."

"But that'll pop it off again."

"That's the point. Do it."

Maisie flung the door open. "Well?"

"*That's it! That's how he knows!*" squealed Glenda. "When somebody opens his door . . . pop! The thread comes off."

"But that's dumb," said Maisie. "He's gotta open the door when *he* comes in here. How's he going to know if he's done it, or if someone else has?"

"Oh, rats! I never thought of that."

"Unless he's a lot smarter than we think," Maisie went on, "and he opens the door just a tiny, little bit—to check if the thread's the way he left it. *Then* he pushes the door wide open."

"Right! *That's* his secret," cried Glenda. "He was fibbing about booby traps."

"And now we can come in here any time we want."

"And bring Marshall with us. To show him a pigsty." Glenda grinned as she looked at the mess. Whew. It was really bad. Lloyd's piles of clothes, towels, magazines, food wrappers, and what-not had grown into mountain ranges since she'd last seen them. "Come on," she said to Maisie. "Let's get the dogs out of here before we lose them."

THAT NIGHT, as the Blumm family sat around the kitchen table having a quick spaghetti dinner, Mrs. Blumm looked at her three children. "What did you all do while Daddy and I were at the store today?"

"Lots," said Honey. "Me and Marshall built us a fort. Then we karate-chopped his shower curtain. Then we dyed Easter eggs and played Chinese checkers. And after that, we made up a new invention."

"What kind of invention?" asked Mr. Blumm.

"We made bowls."

"Bowls aren't new," said Lloyd.

"Ours are. We made them out of grapefruits," said Honey. "We cut them in half and scooped all the stuff out. Then we froze them in the freezer. And tomorrow we're gonna eat soup out of them."

"What about you?" Mrs. Blumm said to Lloyd. "What did you do today?"

"Not much. Like I met some guys for pizza. Then we bought records. I got the new Billy Sundae album . . . *Zinger*."

"*Zinger*, huh?" Mr. Blumm sprinkled grated cheese on his spaghetti. "We can hardly wait to hear it."

"And what about you, Maisie?"

"Glenda and I worked in our office. We finished our newspaper."

"Did you say anything about my room?" asked Lloyd.

"Nope. Not a thing," said Maisie.

•Chapter 7•

IT WAS five-fifteen Sunday morning when Maisie heard Honey knock on her door.

"Go away," Maisie groaned, half asleep. "It's still nighttime."

The door creaked open and Honey came in. "No, it isn't. It's morning. *Easter* morning," she said, pulling Maisie's yellow flowered comforter off her bed. "Don't you want to see what's in our baskets?"

Maisie sat up, rubbing her eyes. "Mom and Dad probably haven't even filled them yet."

"Sure they have . . . I mean *he* has," said Honey. "I heard him hippety-hopping around the house at midnight."

Maisie turned on her bedside lamp, then got out of bed and put on her furry bear slippers. She'd stopped believing in the Easter Bunny a long time ago, and so had Honey. But every year at this time, they became believers again. They put out their baskets, left notes for the Easter Bunny, and never let on for a second—at least in front of their parents—that they'd stopped believing in him.

"If Lloyd wasn't so dumb, he'd still be pretending," Honey whispered as they went downstairs.

Maisie nodded. Lloyd stopped when he was twelve and he hadn't put out his basket since.

"I know I'm going to. Even when I'm married," Honey said.

They both looked at each other and smiled when they went into the den. The plate of cookies they'd left on the coffee table was gone and so were their notes and baskets. This was part of the Easter ritual in the Blumm house. Mr. and Mrs. Blumm always ate the cookies and kept the notes, then they filled the baskets with green cellophane grass, chocolate bunnies, dyed eggs, and lots of little surprises, and hid them behind the couch.

Honey was first to look. "Guess what? The Easter Bunny's trying to fool us this year. He hid them someplace else."

Maisie, who thought Honey was joking, looked behind the couch, fully expecting to find their old straw baskets. "That's funny. They've always been there," she said. "For as long as I can remember." She glanced around the den, thinking. "Maybe they're behind the piano."

"Nope. I already looked," said Honey.

The two girls nearly turned the room upside down, searching for their baskets. They looked under the couch, under the cushions, behind the drapes, inside the TV cabinet, and on top of the bookcase, which was so high up they had to stand on the piano bench to reach it. Then, finally, they dug through six little drawers in the bottom of the curio cabinet, even though they both knew the drawers were too tiny to hold baskets.

"Know what I'll bet," Honey said when they were finished. "I'll bet old rat Lloyd stole them and ate our bunnies."

Maisie shook her head. "Uh-uh, he wouldn't. He thinks chocolate gives him zits."

"*Then where are they?*"

"Maybe they're in the living room. Let's look."

By six o'clock, when the sun was coming up, they'd combed through every room in the house except the four bedrooms.

"Well, we know they're not in mine," said Maisie. "We would've seen them when I turned on my light."

"And they're sure not in mine," said Honey.

"And they wouldn't be in Mom and Dad's."

"*See?* What'd I tell you?" barked Honey. "Old dirty rat Lloyd *did* steal them!"

She was set to march upstairs, that instant, and squirt maple syrup in his hair while he was sleeping, but Maisie wasn't ready to give up their search. Not yet.

"We ought to check out the garage and basement first," she said.

Honey squinched up her eyes. "Okay. But if we *don't* find them . . ."

Their baskets weren't in the garage or the car. To make sure, they looked on the luggage rack, under the hood, and opened the trunk to inspect behind the spare tire. Next they went downstairs and searched every square inch of the basement, including the boiler room and dank, dark corners where there was nothing but mildew and water-bugs.

Honey mumbled to herself all the way back upstairs. "I'm not just gonna squirt syrup in his hair, I'm gonna stuff Crisco up his nose and then . . ."

"There's one last place," Maisie said, leading her through the kitchen. "The screen porch."

". . . I'm gonna sprinkle him with Corn Flakes," Honey continued, "and karate-chop his ears off!"

The door to the porch had been left open and Maisie walked in. "Aha! There's a clue . . . Easter basket grass," she said, pointing to a clump on the flagstone floor.

"And here's another clue," Honey said, stooping down to pick up a jelly bean.

A few feet past the first jelly bean was a second

jelly bean. And a few feet beyond that was Oxie, lying on his back with his front paws curled on his chest, sleeping under a table. Red, yellow, green, and orange Life Savers were stuck in a ring around his mane like beads on a necklace, and he was snoring contentedly with his head between the two overturned, chewed-up Easter baskets.

"Oxie, you rat! You . . . you squirrel-tailed baboon!" Honey shrieked as she and Maisie dug through the remains to see if he'd eaten their chocolate bunnies. "You bum! You schnook! You . . ."

Oxie opened one eye, looked at the two of them, closed his eye, and went on snoring.

"Here's part of a bunny," said Maisie. "He ate the head."

Honey sobbed when Maisie held it up. "That must be yours," she said, and kept digging through the debris, hoping to find the other bunny in one piece. "Oxie, you *bat* brain!" she screamed when she found it. "*All that's left is the rear end!*"

Mixed in with broken eggshells and shreds of cellophane grass were a few pieces of bubble gum with tooth marks, and a variety of half-eaten or well-licked candy. Nothing was worth eating. But each girl managed to find a deck of untouched playing cards and a plastic charm bracelet.

Honey stopped crying when she clasped her bracelet around her wrist. "I guess we can still wear them to church," she sniffed. "Only a few charms are missing."

LATER that morning when Maisie sat in her Sunday school class, she had a hard time concentrating on the Easter lesson her teacher was giving. Her mind was on Oxie. No matter how mad she was at him, she was still curious to know how he'd carried two full baskets out to the porch without leaving a trail of candy through the hall and kitchen. If he'd dropped something, he wouldn't have gone back to pick it up. Oxie wasn't that kind of dog. He was never neat. And he certainly wasn't graceful.

So *how* had he done it?

Maisie thought about it through the rest of her class and during the hymns and Easter sermon afterwards. There was only one explanation. Oxie must have carried the baskets out to the porch one at a time, by gripping their handles between his teeth. Not a bad trick. Nope. Not bad at all.

"What're *you* smiling about?" Honey asked her, as the Blumms got in their car to drive home from church.

"Just Oxie."

"Oh, *him*! Well, I'm not talking to him for two years. And I told him so."

Lloyd, who looked almost unrecognizable with his hair combed and a suit on, climbed in the back seat next to Honey and buried his face in his hands. "*Oh, boo-hoo.* Poor Oxie," he said, pretending he was crying. "Poor old feller. You're gonna die of a broken heart . . . Honey's not talking to you."

"*Mom!*"

"Lloyd, you stop that," said Mrs. Blumm. "You know how upset she is."

"*Boo-hoo. Poor Oxie.*"

Maisie stayed out of their fight and looked out the window. She was thinking of more than Oxie. She was thinking of the Deer Creek Dog Show. And the more she thought about it, the more she smiled. The judges were going to be so impressed when they saw Oxie parade around with a basket, he'd win a blue ribbon for sure. And the best part was, it was a trick she wouldn't have to teach him. He already knew how to do it.

She didn't breathe a word of her secret plan to Glenda when they rode their bikes up and down the street that afternoon, delivering the second edition of *The Poppin Road Gazette*. And she was still keeping it a secret when spring vacation was over and they were back in school.

By then, several weeks had passed since the Fairview School birthday party, and over a hundred students had received letters from people who found balloons. As the letters came in, they were posted on the bulletin board outside Dr. Scotch's office. When there was no space left on the bulletin board, they were taped to the walls along the main corridor.

Of all the letters received, Benedict's was the longest. He'd heard from a dairy farmer in upstate New York, who sent him three type-written pages explaining the process of pasteurizing and bottling milk. Steven, in Maisie's class, had received the shortest. He'd been hoping to hear from someone on a Coast Guard ship, but got four sentences from a first-grader who lived a few miles north of Deer Creek. She sent him a picture she'd drawn of her gerbil and a baby tooth.

Every day Honey looked in the mailbox and said, "Blast it!" when she didn't find a letter. But Maisie and Glenda weren't at all concerned. They were both sure that the longer they waited, the farther their balloons were traveling. Marshall, on the other hand, simply didn't care. He'd been mad at Dr. Scotch the day of the send-off, hadn't expected a letter, and didn't think about it. So he couldn't have been more surprised, one day, when he, Glenda, Maisie, and Honey were playing Slapjack in the Jaxes' kitchen, and his mother hollered that he was wanted on the phone.

Marshall picked up the extension in the kitchen and his end of the conversation went like this:

"Hello . . . Uh-huh, I'm Marshall. . . . Eight."

"No, you're not!" cut in Glenda. "You're still seven."

Marshall turned his back to her. "Almost eight," he said into the phone. "In second grade . . . Yeah? Where was it?"

There was a long pause while he listened.

"I think so. Isn't that one of those roosters that the wind spins around?"

There was another long pause, followed by several "uh-huhs." Then finally he said, "Yeah, I've been there lots of times. It's next to the drugstore. . . . The ones with meatballs. . . . Nope, I hate Coke. I only like root beer."

Maisie, Glenda, and Honey were glued to their seats, hanging on to every word.

"Who was that?" Glenda asked when he hung up.

"The man who owns the Downtown Deli," said Marshall.

"Mr. Abruzzio?"

Marshall nodded.

"What'd he want?"

"He didn't want anything."

"Then why was he calling?" asked Maisie.

"To tell me he found my balloon."

"Where'd he find it?" asked Honey.

"On his roof."

"*What? Here in Deer Creek?*" bellowed Maisie.

"How'd it keep from falling off?" Honey asked.

"Never mind that," said Glenda. "How come he asked if you knew where his deli was?"

Marshall, who never liked to volunteer much information and thought three or four words were enough to answer any question, sat back down at the table. "Who's turn is it to deal?"

"Hey! Now wait a minute," Glenda said, grabbing the cards out of his hands. "If Mr. Abruzzio called to tell you he found your balloon, then why were you talking about meatballs?"

"Yeah, and Cokes and root beers," said Honey.

"And how come he didn't see your balloon a long time ago?" asked Maisie.

Marshall was trapped. He'd been winning at Slapjack and wanted to go on playing, but the three of them refused. "Not till you tell us every word Mr. Abruzzio said . . . from the beginning," said Glenda.

Marshall sighed. "Okay. First he asked if I was Marshall Jax."

"Skip that. Get to the part about the balloon."

Marshall sighed again. "He said he found it

when he was up on his roof cleaning his gutters . . ."

"Which roof? The one on his house or the one on his deli?"

"On his house."

"Go on."

"The string was caught on his weather vane. And the balloon was shrunk. But my letter wasn't wrecked."

"Of course not. He couldn't have called if it had been," said Glenda. "Now get to the point. What about the meatballs?"

Marshall rubbed his nose. "He asked what kind of hero sandwiches I like. So I told him the ones with meatballs."

"Then what?"

"He said I could come to his deli any time I wanted . . ."

"Yes?"

". . . and bring two friends. He'd treat us."

"But there are *three* of us," said Maisie.

"That's okay," said Glenda. "He and Honey can share a hero."

Marshall stuck his chin out. "No, we won't! Honey gets a *whole* hero. She's my friend. But you and Maisie don't get anything."

"Why, Marshykins . . . how can you say that? Maisie and I love you! We adore you! We worship the ground you walk on," cooed Glenda, placing her hands on her heart.

"We even love to kiss the air you breathe," Maisie said, leaning across the table and going *smack, smack* around his head.

"You don't keep promises," he said.

"What promises?" asked Maisie.

"Glenda knows."

"Oh, *that* promise." Glenda forced a laugh. "Well, Maisie and I wanted to make it a surprise. But now I guess we'll have to tell you. The day *after* we all go to the deli, we're taking you to see a pigsty."

Marshall shook his head. "Nope, before. *Today*. As soon as we play another game of Slapjack."

Glenda and Maisie looked at each other in disbelief. He'd outfoxed them. Now what?

"Hmm. We're not sure if we can," said Glenda. "We don't know where the farmer is." She tapped Maisie's foot under the table. "Do you know if the—*ahem*—farmer is in or out?"

Maisie glanced at the clock over the sink. "The *ahem* farmer's supposed to be downtown with his mother getting a haircut and a new tennis racket."

"That's funny." Honey laughed. "Lloyd's doing the same thing."

"So if we're going, we'll have to leave now."

With the pleased look of someone who thinks

he's got the upper hand, Marshall stood up and put his hands on his hips. "Okay, we'll go now. And *Honey* is coming with us!"

"Hmm, I don't know," said Glenda.

"Well-l," said Maisie.

They hemmed and hawed, pretending they were making an earth-shaking decision, even though they'd known all along Honey had to come. If she didn't, and she went home, she'd be in the house when they took Marshall there anyway.

"We're going to have to step out in the hall a minute to talk it over," said Maisie.

When she and Glenda came back into the kitchen, Maisie sighed as if they'd given in. "Okay, Marshall, you win. Honey can come. But *only* on two conditions. First, you have to sign a contract—a piece of paper that says even if you don't *like* the pigsty, you still have to take me and Glenda to the deli."

"What's the other one?" asked Marshall.

Glenda opened a drawer and pulled out two dish towels. "We'll tell you when we're ready to leave."

·Chapter 8·

"*WALK?* How can we *walk* to a farm?" howled Honey.

"It's a very close farm," said Maisie. "Now stand still while I fix your blindfold."

"I don't like this come-dishion," said Marshall.

Glenda was firm. "Tough. You want to see a pigsty?" she said as she tied a dish towel around his head. "Then you wear it."

Once the dish towels were securely knotted, she and Maisie spun Honey and Marshall around three times for good measure, then gave them one last piece of advice: If they passed any neighbors on their way to the farm, and the neighbors wanted to know where they were going, they had to say nowhere; they were just playing a game.

"That's because," said Maisie, "if they find out we're going to see a pigsty, they'll beg to come with us."

Glenda opened the door, then she and Maisie

took Marshall and Honey by the hand and led them down the steps and out the front walk. But instead of going directly across the street to the Blumms' house, they turned left and went all the way to the bottom of the hill; then back up again, making broad loops and zigzags, the purpose of which was to keep Honey and Marshall from guessing they were still on Poppin Road.

"How much farther is it?" Marshall complained while they were circling the Klines' yard.

"Not too far," said Maisie. "Now watch your feet. There's a big cowpie in front of you."

Marshall took little mincing steps sideways. "Am I in it?"

"Nope, you're doing just fine," said Glenda.

"Am I?" said Honey.

"Terrific," said Maisie. "Now you and Marshall stand right where you are a second. Glenda and I have to open a gate . . . there's a hen house up ahead."

Honey and Marshall clutched each other's hands and Maisie and Glenda dashed up to a maple tree, ducked behind it, and started going, "*Pluck, pluck, pluck, pluck, squawk, squawkkkk! Pluck, pluck, pluck, pluck . . .*"

"Why, hello there, hens," said Glenda. "I see you're laying eggs."

"*Plop, plop, pop, plop,*" went Maisie.

"*Crr-eeeakk,*" went Glenda. "Boy! Heavy gate. Okay, guys! Gate's open. We're coming back for you."

"Why can't we see the chickens?" Honey asked, once Maisie had her by the hand again.

"Maybe next time," said Maisie. "We told the farmer we were only coming to see his sty."

"*Mooooo! Mooooo!*" went Glenda.

"That was you!" said Marshall.

"Of course it was," she said. "I was talking to that cow in the pasture."

"*Mooooo! Mooooo!*" went Maisie deep in her throat, with her hand cupped over her mouth.

"That was the cow answering," said Glenda.

"It sounded real close, Marshall," said Honey.

"When're we getting to the pigs?" he said.

"Soon," said Glenda.

When they'd zigzagged Poppin Road twice more and were on the Blumms' side again, Maisie said they were passing a haystack and way out yonder, in a field, she could see the farmer riding his tractor.

"Looks like he got a good haircut," said Glenda.

"Come on, guys. Wave. Wave to Farmer Brown," said Maisie. "He's waving at us."

Honey waved, but Marshall refused to because he was wearing a blindfold and couldn't see Farmer Brown. He was also acting a little bit irritable—

as if he wasn't completely convinced he was on a real farm.

"If I am," he said, "why do I keep feeling streets?"

"Because this is a *modern* farm," explained Maisie, who just that moment saw Mr. Larsen come out of his garage wheeling his lawn mower. "They even use lawn mowers to cut the hay," she said, poking Glenda and pointing to Mr. Larsen.

"Well, I'll be darned . . . there's a farmhand ready to mow hay right now," said Glenda. "Hi, there!" she hollered down the street.

"Hi, kids," Mr. Larsen called back.

"You getting ready to mow?"

"Sure am," called Mr. Larsen.

"What a nice, friendly farmhand," Maisie said.

Marshall perked up when he heard the *putt-putt* of the lawnmower. "Couldn't we just watch a minute?"

"Nope. It's not part of the deal," said Glenda. "Anyway, we're almost up to the pig house. Wait right there while Maisie and I open the door."

She and Maisie quickly ran across the Blumms' yard and opened the front door. "*Oinnkk, oinnkk, oinnkk,*" they snorted together. The sound immediately brought Oxie flying through the house to meet them.

Maisie grabbed his collar. "You go back and get Honey and Marshall," she said loud enough for them to hear. "And I'll wait here to make sure this—*ahem*—pig doesn't get loose."

Honey and Marshall both had smiles as big as bananas beneath their blindfolds when Glenda led them into the house. By then, Maisie had shut Oxie in the den and found a sour-smelling sponge in the kitchen.

"Sure smells of pigs in here, doesn't it?" she said, passing the sponge under Honey and Marshall's noses.

"Smells more like stinky feet to me," said Honey.

"Can we take off our blindfolds?" asked Marshall.

"Not till we get to the second floor, where the pigsty is," said Glenda.

Honey was so excited, she didn't recognize the feel of her own house. And if Marshall noticed things like a clock ticking or carpet under his feet, he didn't comment.

"Almost there," Maisie kept saying on their way upstairs, "almost there."

At the landing, Glenda gave her Marshall's hand to hold and hurried on ahead to Lloyd's room, where she felt under his door for the secret thread. She carefully untaped it, pushed the door wide open and called, "Ready!" Then she started giggling.

When Maisie led Honey and Marshall into the

room, *she* started giggling. Good old predictable Lloyd! He couldn't have left a worse mess if he'd hired a bulldozer.

"*Ta dum!*" she said. "Welcome to a pigsty."

Marshall crunched across a trail of corn chips and Honey bumped into an open drawer, too heaped with unmatched socks to slide back into the dresser.

"Help! What's that? . . .What am I stepping on? A pig?" she screeched when she brought her foot smack down on a drawer that was lying on the floor.

"Take off your blindfolds and see," said Maisie.

Marshall ripped his off at the same time as Honey. He stared. And she stared. His mouth hung open. Hers looked like the Grand Canyon. Then, without giving any warning, she whirled around with her hand flying through the air like a Ping-Pong paddle, aiming for Maisie.

"This was a trick! A lousy, scuzzy trick!" she shouted, as Maisie ducked to avoid getting a karate chop. "You didn't take us to a farm! You brought us to Lloyd's room!"

Marshall wasn't at all upset. He seemed fascinated. "*Lloyd lives here?*"

"You know he does! You've been in here before," Honey said, mad at him now. "Remember?"

Marshall shook his head.

"Well, you have!"

"No, I haven't!"

"You *have!*"

"*Haven't!* Lloyd never lets anyone in."

Honey's Ping-Pong hand was ready to give him a karate chop when he stepped around a mound of soda cans stacked into a four-foot pyramid. "What's that?" he asked.

"What's what?"

"That thing there," he said, pointing to the black box with the green light blipping across a panel.

Honey's hand fell. "I don't know. What is it, Maisie?"

"Some kind of alarm system," Maisie invented on the spot. "It's sort of like a fire alarm. Only this is a *mess* alarm. When Lloyd's room gets dangerous to his health, a red light goes on."

"Then what happens?"

"I guess everything blows up."

Honey snatched Marshall's arm. "Come on, Marsh . . . let's leave. *Now!*"

He shrugged her hand off. "Not yet. I want to know where Lloyd sleeps."

"In his bed," said Glenda.

"Well, *where* is it?"

Glenda nodded toward a tower of crumpled

sheets and blankets, heaped pillows, damp towels, dirty clothes, strewn comics, books, records, magazines, assorted sports equipment, and crushed, empty cookie boxes. "Under there somewhere," she said. "I think."

Maisie, meanwhile, had made her way across the room. "Anybody want to see Lloyd's calendar? It's got a picture of a girl hatching out of an egg."

As she was talking, there was a low rumble that came from the road, went up the driveway, grew louder and louder in the garage underneath them, shook the floor, and ran up the walls of the room.

Honey glanced at the black box to see if the light was red. "See, Maisie? You were wrong! It's *green* when the room blows up!"

Maisie put her finger to her lips. "*Sshh!* Listen!" One car door slammed, then another. "Mom and Lloyd are home! Quick! Honey, you and Marshall run to my room and stay there," she said. "Glenda and I'll be right in. We have to fix something."

Honey bolted out first, knocking over Lloyd's four-foot pyramid of soda cans, and Marshall tore out after her. "We don't have time to stack the cans. Leave them," Glenda said to Maisie. "Lloyd'll think the wind blew them over."

No sooner had they taped the secret thread back in place and were hurrying down the hall, than Mrs. Blumm called upstairs, "Hi, we're back. Anybody home?"

Maisie and Glenda quickly ducked in the hall bathroom and turned on both sink faucets full blast. "We are . . . Glenda and me," Maisie called over the rising steam. "We're washing our hands."

"Where's Honey?"

"In my room with Marshall. They're studying their times tables."

"They're what? I can't hear you?"

"*Studying their times tables.*"

"You believe that, Ma, you'll believe anything," Lloyd said as he hopped upstairs.

Maisie and Glenda listened to his footsteps as he turned down the hall, and continued lathering their hands, which were covered with a good, thick, creamy layer of pink soap by the time he came by the bathroom.

"If you've been in my room, I'll know," he said, stopping outside to watch them.

Maisie passed the bar of soap to Glenda, who lathered up to her elbows and passed it back to her. "Who'd *want* to go in your room?" she said, looking up at him in the foggy mirror and passing the soap back to Glenda.

"*You* would, bimbo. And if you have been, you're dead!"

They held their breath, rinsing. One, two, three,

four . . . he was up to his door. Good. No fuss. They kept rinsing and waiting. Still no fuss. He must not have noticed the cans. . . .

Ya upt 'n left me . . . ya thumbed yer nose,
'N now ah'm wiltin' like a poooor crushed rose. . . .
Oh yeah, bam boom

blasted his stereo.

They stopped rinsing and dried their hands, which were puckered as new seersucker. Then they darted out of the bathroom and down the hall, the other way, to Maisie's room.

"Seven times seven," Honey was saying.

"Fourteen," answered Marshall.

"Excellent. Now six times three."

"Nine."

"Perfect. Now five times eight."

Marshall looked up at Maisie and Glenda when they came in. "See? We *are* practicing our times tables."

"Does Lloyd know we were in his room?" said Honey.

Maisie shook her head, then told Honey and Marshall to stand up and place their hands on her yellow address book. "You're going to take a vow—that's a sacred promise you can't break unless you want lightning to strike you on the head and make all your hair fall out. Even your eyebrows. Now repeat after me," she said. "I swear to God . . ."

"*I swear to God . . .*"

"I'll never ever tell Lloyd I was snooping in his room . . ."

"*I'll never ever tell Lloyd I was snooping in his room . . .*"

"And if I do . . ."

"*And if I do . . .*"

"I swear I'll never ever tell who took me in there . . ."

"*I swear I'll never ever tell who took me in there . . .*"

". . . even at gunpoint."

"*. . . even at gunpoint.*"

THEIR lips were sealed. Not a word was mentioned about pigsties or anything else that could be connected, in any way, to their visit to Lloyd's room.

Or so Maisie and Glenda thought.

As far as they were concerned, they'd made a promise and they'd kept it. Now it was up to Marshall to keep his promise—to take them to the Downtown Deli. As a reminder, they made the following public announcement in *The Poppin Road Gazette*:

NEIGHBORHOOD BOY WINS FREE HEROES

You never know what you'll find on your roof when you clean your gutters these days. Mr. Abruzzio, the owner of the Downtown Deli, found a balloon with a letter on his. Who'd the balloon belong to? Poppin Road's very own Marshall Jax.

As a treat, Mr. Abruzzio has invited Marshall to come to the deli and bring two friends for free heroes and sodas. When our reporters interviewed Marshall, he said he was definitely inviting his sister, Glenda, and her friend, Maisie Blumm and maybe Maisie's sister, Honey. Don't forget, Marshall!

The Editors

◆Chapter 9◆

THE DATE was set. They were going to the deli
Wednesday afternoon, right after Honey and
Marshall's weekly peewee karate lesson, and Mrs.
Jax was driving.

Before they left, Marshall gave Maisie and
Glenda a contract to sign:

1) They couldn't watch the karate lesson.
2) They had to share a hero and soda.

Maisie and Glenda signed.

They brought their cash box with the $18.75
they'd saved from selling ads for *The Poppin Road
Gazette*, and as soon as Mrs. Jax parked her blue
station wagon in front of the Y, they got out and
walked four doors down Main Street to the Town
Clerk's Office.

The clerk's assistant, a tall, thin woman with a
crane neck and funny little glasses that looked

cut in half, saw them and came over to the counter where they were waiting. "You're here to register for the Deer Creek Dog Show?"

Maisie and Glenda nodded.

The woman gave each of them a pink entry form to fill out. "The fee's two dollars," she said. "And this year we've got five categories. You can enter your dogs in as many as you want."

She went back to her desk while Maisie and Glenda wrote in their names, addresses, phone numbers, and dogs' names, and read the rules, prize list, and categories to check.

☐ 1. Smallest Dog   ☐ 3. Best Trick
☐ 2. Biggest Dog   ☐ 4. Most Beautiful
           ☐ 5. Most Intelligent

Maisie checked the box for Best Trick and was just about to check the one for Most Beautiful when Glenda peeked over at her entry form.

"Best Trick? Why'd you sign Oxie up for that?"

"Because he does a good one."

"I never saw him."

"Doesn't mean he can't."

"Doesn't mean he can, either!"

"You'll see. It's better than anything Snookums does!"

"Snookums doesn't *need* to do tricks! She'll probably win for Most Beautiful."

"Ha! The way her fur's matted?"

"You wait till I *groom* her! *She's* a registered purebred!"

"Purebred what? Purebred dust mop?"

"AKC . . . American Kennel Club purebred! Her grandfather was a *very* famous champion."

"What was her grandmother? *A bird's nest?*"

"Ask me, *anything's* better than being a big old dumb ox with a squirr—"

"*Ah-hmph!*"

Maisie and Glenda glanced over at the woman with the funny half glasses. "Are you girls finished?" she asked.

They quickly filled out the rest of their entry forms, left them on the counter with four dollars from their cash box, then stalked out of the Town Clerk's Office and down the street toward the car, staying far apart from each other.

Maisie was in the lead with a smug smile on her face. Their friendship was over, for sure, but this time it didn't matter so much. She had something she knew must be killing Glenda. *She* had the cash box. One half of the $14.75 left in there belonged to Glenda. And she knew Glenda was itching to spend it.

She walked faster, keeping ahead. There were several things she could do. She could disappear in a store and let Glenda think she was spending *all* the money. Or she could walk around the block for an hour, making Glenda follow her. Or she could sit in the car with the doors locked so Glenda couldn't get in. Or . . .

Without any warning, the cash box was ripped out from under her arm. She turned, screaming, and saw the thief streak past her. Glenda! And *she* was heading for the car.

"Oh, no you don't!"

Glenda cut around an old woman pushing a grocery cart and Maisie cut around the woman the other way, catching up with Glenda just as she reached for the door handle. "I had that! Give it back!"

"Try and get it!"

Glenda shot around the front of the car, going for the driver's side, and Maisie wheeled around from the rear. She lunged for the cash box, missed it, and lunged again, knocking Glenda off balance. As Glenda slammed against the fender, the cash box flew out of her hand and landed in the street.

Barrrromp-ponkk!

Both girls looked up. A tractor-trailer truck— one of the big ones with more tires than a centipede has feet—was rumbling down Main Street. Maisie let out a long, low wail along with Glenda. A truck tire ran over the cash box. Then another. And another . . .

Quarters, nickels, and dimes shot up in the air, scattering every which way.

When the last tire rolled on by, Maisie saw a green bill that was stuck to a tread roll along with it. "There goes all our money," she bawled.

"Maybe not," cried Glenda. "Maybe some's left. Let's look."

While Maisie searched along the gutters for coins, Glenda waited until she was sure there was no more traffic, then dashed out to the street to bring back their cash box.

"I found a few nickels and two quarters," Maisie called. "What did you find?"

"I don't know yet."

Glenda ran up to the curb, trying to pull apart something smashed beyond recognition. "Who'd believe this used to be a nice cigar box?" she cried when Maisie ran over to help her.

One end was ripped off, and they knew that's where their money had come out. It wouldn't open there, so they both dug their nails under the crushed lid and pulled. Inside, untouched, were three dimes, a five-dollar bill and two singles.

"I guess our other five was what stuck to the truck tire," Maisie said.

Glenda nodded.

They didn't know whether to keep crying because so much was gone, or laugh because so much was still there.

"How much did you say you found in the gutter?"

Maisie looked in her hand. "Seventy cents."

"Let's see. Seventy cents plus seven dollars and thirty cents in the cash box is eight dollars," said Glenda. "And five dollars on the tire makes thirteen. That means . . ."

". . . we've got a dollar seventy-five lying around here somewhere."

They found a nickel and two dimes under the car parked in front of the Jaxes' station wagon, and another dime on the curb across the street, which they kept even though they weren't really sure it was theirs. Then Glenda saw a quarter in some muck under a sewer grate.

"I think we ought to leave it and spend what we've got," she said, "before anything else happens."

Maisie agreed. She looked up at the clock with the Roman numerals over the bank. It was four-thirty-five. "Where do you want to go?" she asked. "We've got twenty-five minutes till we have to be at the deli."

"Woolworth's?"

They combed the aisles like two professional shoppers and came out eleven minutes later with

an assortment of fruit-scented stickers, a folding
pocket hairbrush for each of them, and nail polish that had been marked down to 3/$1.00. They
selected Eggyolk, Blueberry Glitter, and Seafoam
Aqua, which they promised they'd take turns
sharing.

Then they hurried back down Main Street and
went into the drugstore. Nobody else was there
except the druggist, who was filling prescriptions
in the rear, so they had the whole long, glass
cosmetics counter to themselves. There were
lighted mirrors, trays of sample lipsticks, testers
of perfume and hand lotions, sample eyeliners,
sample blushes, sample eye shadows, and samples
of things they'd never even heard of.

While Glenda did her eyes, Maisie moisturized
her face and brushed highlighter on her cheeks.
"Don't you feel like you're in heaven?" she said,
reaching for the lipsticks.

Glenda smiled at herself in a mirror and flut-
tered her multi-colored eyelids. "I'll bet heaven
isn't half as fun."

For the next seven or eight minutes they sam-
pled everything they thought smelled or looked
good. Then Glenda had a feeling their time was
running out. And here they were—with five dollars they hadn't spent.

She looked at the items on the novelty rack and

Maisie scanned the shelves with suntan lotions until a tube called E-Z Bronze Gel caught her eye. She picked it up, read how the gel could give a deep tan without sun, then brought the tube over to Glenda.

"What do you think?"

Glenda read the price. "We should definitely get it."

It was four seventy-five. With the tax added on, it would use up the rest of their money.

"You girls must've had a good time in here," the druggist said when they paid for it.

"Oh, we did," said Maisie.

"A ball," said Glenda. "Your cosmetics counter is one of our most favorite places in town."

"So I see."

When they breezed into the deli next door, feeling glamorous, Marshall and Honey were sitting in a booth talking to Mr. Abruzzio, the owner, and Mrs. Jax was waiting for them just inside the doorway.

"Where on *earth* . . .?"

"Isn't it terrific, Mom?" said Glenda. "And it was all *free*! Even the tattoos."

"*What* tattoos?"

"Show her yours first, Maisie."

Maisie proudly extended her arm. "It's a fish," she said, displaying a puff-bellied creature she'd drawn between her wrist and her elbow using blue eyeliner.

"Mine's up higher. On my shoulder," Glenda said, lifting her shirt sleeve. "A crab. And the lipstick's called Fire Engine Red. See? It matches my lips."

When Mrs. Jax didn't say anything, Glenda groaned.

"Jeez, Mom . . . don't you *get* it? A *fish* and a *crab*! Those are our *signs*! You know . . . the zodiac?"

Mrs. Jax shoved the door open. "Just go eat your heroes!" she said. "I'll be back later . . . I've got marketing to do."

Marshall and Honey, who were showing Mr. Abruzzio how they tied their belts around their white karate suits, looked up and stared as Maisie and Glenda came over to their booths.

"Yuck," said Honey. "Where've *you* been?"

"Is there a fair in town?" asked Mr. Abruzzio.

"Not that I know of . . . we've been at the drugstore," Glenda said, trying to slide in next to Marshall.

He put his foot up, blocking her. "Nope. You can't sit here. Not with that goop on your face."

"Revlon does *not* make goop. Now move over!"

Maisie slid in next to Honey, who immediately pinched her nose. "Eww. You stink!"

"Stink! How can you say that? This is Rhapsody . . . a very expensive toilet water."

"*Toilet* water?"

". . . I'm warning you, Marshall. Put it down or I'm knocking it down."

"Nope." He twisted his face into his fiercest karate expression and held up his hands.

"Hey, kids . . . stop! Please. No hitting in the deli . . . Marshall! Girls!"

The four of them looked up at Mr. Abruzzio, who was mopping a bald spot on his head with a hankie.

"There. Much better. Now. How does *four* heroes, *four* sodas, and *four* Italian ices for dessert sound?"

They all smiled. "Wow. Sounds good," said Glenda, pushing Marshall's foot out of her way.

While they were eating, Honey stopped pinching her nose because it plugged up her ears, and Marshall gradually warmed up to Maisie and Glenda's makeup.

"Show me your tattoos again," he said.

Maisie extended her arm and Glenda lifted her shirt sleeve.

"Will you make me one?"

"Depends on how fast you eat," said Glenda. "If we're out of here before Mom comes, we might have time."

"You'll do it at the drugstore?"

She nodded.

Maisie had a better idea. She reached in the brown shopping bag from Woolworth's and took out the three bottles of nail polish. "We can do it right here with these," she said, setting the bottles on the table.

"What about me? I want a tattoo," said Honey.

Maisie took a bite of her salami and cheese hero. "Okay. Pick a color."

Honey chose Blueberry Glitter and Marshall chose Seafoam Aqua. Then Glenda stroked the outline of a scorpion on the back of his hand and Maisie started a goat on Honey's arm.

"What's that?" she said.

"A goat."

"I don't want a goat. I want a horse."

"You can't," said Maisie. "A goat's your sign."

"I want a horse anyway."

Maisie dipped the brush back into the Blueberry Glitter and made a long tail on the end of the goat. "There you go . . . a horse."

Honey was satisfied, but Marshall wasn't. "My scorpion looks like Maisie's fish," he said.

"That's because Maisie's fish looks like a scorpion," said Glenda.

Maisie crunched on an ice cube from her soda glass. "No, it doesn't. Your scorpion looks like *my* fish."

"Oh, yeah?" Glenda grabbed Marshall's hand.

"Look at this!" she said, making something that looked like a large string bean with a dagger on the tip. "A tail with a stinger! Tell me *that* doesn't look like a scorpion!"

"Ha ha ha ha . . ."

Mr. Abruzzio whisked a tray with four paper cups up to their booth just then. "Here we go . . . dessert," he said, handing each of them a raspberry ice. "Specialty of the house."

"Oh, boy . . . double scoops!" said Honey.

Glenda smiled like an angel. "Why, thank you very, very much, Mr. Abruzzio."

"This was just about the best dinner we ever had," Maisie added, sweet as sugar.

"You're a nice man," said Marshall.

THEY were all in high spirits, standing in front of the deli, licking their ices, when Mrs. Jax pulled up in the station wagon. Marshall climbed into the back seat first.

"What's on your forehead?" his mother asked him.

"A sticker. It smells like watermelon when you scratch it."

Glenda, Maisie, and Honey piled in after him, plastered with fruit stickers. "Aren't they neat, Mom?" said Glenda. "Maze and I bought them at Woolworth's."

"And guess what they made me and Marsh tattoos with?" said Honey.

"Never mind . . . I'd rather not know," Mrs. Jax said. She heaved a sigh as she started away from the curb, and that was the last sound they heard from her the whole trip home.

When Maisie and Honey went in their house, Mrs. Blumm wasn't much more talkative. She was wearing an old sweatshirt and faded jeans, sweeping the corners of the living room ceiling with a broom wrapped in a towel, and frowning.

"What're you doing?" asked Maisie.

"Going after cobwebs."

"Why? Are we having company?"

"No, we're not having company!"

Bar-rummm, bar-rummm. They heard a vacuum upstairs.

"Who's up there?"

"Lloyd is. He's cleaning his room. And I *do* mean *cleaning* it!"

Maisie and Honey eyed each other. They each had a funny feeling something was up.

"I thought you said if he wanted to live in a junkyard, it was his business, not yours," said Honey. "I heard you."

"Well, I was wrong!"

"Did you go in his room?" asked Maisie.

"You bet I did! Right after all the little Larsen boys were here this afternoon, I—" Mrs. Blumm interrupted herself, listening to someone clomp downstairs. "Is that you, Lloyd?"

He appeared at the bottom of the stairs, on his way to the laundry room with a huge basket of dirty clothes. His face was hidden behind it.

"*Get every sock, every towel, every shirt, sheet, and pillowcase on your floor! Do you hear me?*" Mrs. Blumm hollered after him.

"Okay, okay. I'm doing it," he whined behind his basket.

"What were you saying about the Larsen boys?" asked Maisie.

Mrs. Blumm leaned her broom against the wall and spritzed glass cleaner on a window. She hadn't noticed how Maisie or Honey looked yet, and they were quickly peeling off their stickers. "The Larsen boys? Oh, yes . . . I was telling you they rang our doorbell this afternoon."

"What for?"

"At first I thought it was to see if Honey could play. But they had a very peculiar request. Robby kept talking about a *pig's eye*! Three or four times he said it . . . would I *please* let them in to see our pig's eye. I had no idea what he wanted until Brett, the oldest one . . ."

This time when Maisie looked at Honey, Honey was watching her feet.

". . . said his little brother meant where a pig

lived. *A pigsty!* They'd heard Lloyd lived in one . . . *can you imagine*?" Mrs. Blumm said, scrubbing furiously at a speck on the window. "Now little children wouldn't dream up a thing like *that*! Somebody's said *something* about our house."

When Maisie cornered Honey alone out in the hall, she said, "All right! Who blabbed? You or Marshall?"

"Well . . ."

"*Who*?"

"Well, we both kinda did. It sort of slipped out."

"I'm telling Mom!"

"Better not," said Honey.

"Oh, yeah. Why?"

"Because then I'll have to tell her and Lloyd how you and Glenda took me and Marshall to see a pig farm."

"Hmm." Maisie reconsidered her threat. "I'll make you a deal. If you won't tell, I won't tell."

"It's a deal."

They shook hands, and as they went upstairs, Maisie said, "Actually, we're doing a good thing by not telling. If we did, we'd just cause trouble."

•Chapter 10•

TOMORROW was Saturday, the day of the Deer Creek Dog Show. *The Poppin Road Gazette* was suspended till further notice and things were tense.

All week long, Glenda had badgered Maisie to tell her what Oxie was doing for Best Trick, but Maisie refused to on the grounds that the trick was "top secret." Sharing it, she said, would jinx it.

To get even with her, Glenda wouldn't tell Maisie how she was grooming Snookums, except to say she'd picked up a few hints from beauty magazines. The tips mostly involved hair.

Their loyalty to their dogs hadn't led to a real fight, but as a matter of principle, they stopped speaking. Their last words to each other were on the bus coming home from school Friday afternoon.

Maisie said: "I hope you know this is *my* week to keep the Seafoam Aqua nail polish."

And Glenda replied: "You can have it as soon as you give me *my* half of the E-Z-Bronze Gel."

The exchange was made at four P.M. by Honey, who delivered to Glenda a measuring cup filled with three ounces of gel—exactly half of what was in the tube—and returned home with what was left of the nail polish. But her *real* mission was to spy.

Maisie stood in the doorway, dying for her to come back so she could hear her report.

"Okay, quick! Tell me . . . what's Glenda doing to Snookums?"

"She wouldn't even let me in the house," said Honey. "I had to stand on the steps."

"Well, did you pump her? Did she say anything?"

"That she'd give me a snickerdoodle if I told her what Oxie's trick was."

"Then what? What did you say?"

"What you told me to. That he was gonna jump through a hoop of fire with a ball balanced on his nose."

"Aha! See there! Do *I* know Glenda?" Maisie said, looking very pleased with herself. "Did I *know* she'd try and bribe you?"

Honey stomped off, not answering, and Maisie called after her. "Hey! Why're you so mad? You got your snickerdoodle, didn't you?"

"Not one bite!" Honey shot over her shoulder. "Glenda said she *knew* you'd put me up to telling her a phony trick."

"What made her think that?"

"Ask her. Not me. She said Oxie was probably dumb enough to jump through fire, but he sure wasn't smart enough to balance a ball on his nose. Then she slammed the door."

Maisie forced a laugh. "Ha ha. His trick's even *better* than balancing a ball."

"Then why won't you tell me?"

"You'll find out tomorrow when the time comes."

"See that! See what you do?" Honey spun around with her eyes squinched up. "You always act like Oxie's *your* dog! Well, he's not! He's *mine*, too, you know. And if he does something, *I* ought to know about it!"

Maisie considered a moment. Maybe she wasn't being fair. "I'll make you a deal," she said. "You help me give him a bath, then I'll tell you what his trick is."

Honey grinned. "You mean he really, truly *does* one?"

Bathing Oxie was no easy task. While his water was running, Honey poured in a bottle of sweet-smelling Carnation bath salts, and Maisie lined up the equipment they'd need: flea shampoo, a scrub brush, anti-tangle conditioner, a bucket for rinse water, and every towel she could find. When the tub was full, the girls put on their swimsuits.

Oxie, meanwhile, was down in the den, curled up snoring on the forbidden couch. He was dreaming of bones, biscuits, and chasing the brown Parcel Post truck—the things he loved most. A familiar jangle woke him up. He popped open one eye and saw Maisie and Honey sneaking up on him with his chain leash. They were up to no good. He knew it. But before he could make a getaway, they snared him and dragged him upstairs to the bathroom. Then they hoisted him into the tub of warm, frothy pink water.

The battle was fierce.

Oxie yelped, howled, splashed, reared like a bronco, shivered, shook, and clawed at the edge of the tub. Finally, Maisie and Honey climbed in with him. Maisie squirted him with dollops of flea shampoo. Honey gripped his collar, wrangling with him as if he were a calf.

"Please," she pleaded. "Please, please, *please* cooperate!"

Oxie would have none of it. He bolted out of the tub, splashing water on the floor, and dashed for the door. Maisie was quicker. She got there ahead of him, by skidding across the wet tile. Then she shut the door. Oxie was trapped.

Twenty minutes later the bathroom looked as

if Hurricane Mary had hit a mudhole, but the job was finished. Oxie was clean. Sweet-smelling carnation clean. Now they had to dry him. They used up the towels, every last one of them, even rolled him in the bath mat, but his drenched coat still clung to his ribs.

"What'll we use on him *now*?" said Honey.

Maisie flicked some dog fur off her lip and stood up. "You get your bedspread and I'll get my brush and blow dryer."

WHEN Mr. Blumm called, "Dinnertime!" both girls were limp with exhaustion. The muscles in their arms and legs ached, and Oxie still needed more work. The bushiest parts of him, his tail and his rear end, had to be brushed out. With that to look forward to, Maisie and Honey were in no mood for Lloyd's jokes about their swimsuits.

"Woo! Woo! Like what've we got here?" he cracked as they sat down to eat. "Two contestants for the Miss Universe pageant?"

Honey told him to watch his mouth *or else* . . . and Maisie ignored him and began eating the slice of steaming lasagna her mother put on her plate. There was nothing she liked better, but she picked at it as if the weight of her fork was too much for her. Whew! Getting ready for a dog show was a lot of hard work. Was it worth it? she wondered. In some ways Glenda was lucky to have a puny dog. All she had to do to bathe Snookums was dunk her in a mixing bowl.

"How're things going?" asked Mrs. Blumm, sitting down.

"With Oxie?" said Honey. "Oh, fine. He's gonna win a blue ribbon for Best Trick tomorrow."

"*Oxie* does a trick?" said Lloyd.

"Yeah, he does!" snapped Honey. "And a darn good one!" Then she looked across the table at Maisie. "Heyyy! You *still* haven't told me what it is."

Maisie wound a piece of stringy mozzarella cheese around her fork. "Later, okay? After we finish his grooming." Then she thought of Oxie's tail and smiled. His beautiful tail. The best-looking part of him. When it was all brushed out, nice and fluffy, he'd be so cute carrying his bask— Basket!! She'd forgotten! She and Honey didn't *have* baskets. He'd chewed them up.

"Lloyd!" she suddenly shrieked. "Your basket! Your old *Easter* basket! *Where is it?*"

"Huh? My basket? Beats me."

"*Think*! Where do you *think* you put it?"

Lloyd shrugged. "In the basement, maybe. Or maybe it was thrown out. I dunno. Haven't seen it in years."

As soon as he said basement, Maisie was up on her feet, racing out of the kitchen.

Honey stared after her. "What's the big fuss about Easter baskets?" she asked. "Easter was last month." Then a funny look crossed her face and suddenly she dropped *her* fork. "*Maaaiisiieee!*"

By this time, Maisie was down in the boiler room, digging through a carton full of old toys and board games. "It's gotta be in here," she was crying. "Gotta be."

"*If Oxie's trick is chewing up a basket . . . you're dead!*" boomed Honey behind her.

Maisie brought her head out of the carton to face two small, but menacing hands chopping the air. "Cut it out," she said, swatting them out of her way. "Of course that's not his trick! He can *carry* a basket."

"You swear?"

Maisie sighed. "Dope! How do you think he got our baskets out on the porch Easter morning?"

"It must've been by . . . *wow*! By carrying them!"

"Right. Now help me find Lloyd's."

IT WAS nowhere to be found. When they gave up looking, they were both in tears. At this hour, there wasn't a store in town open, and even if one was, it wouldn't be selling Easter baskets. Not eleven months before Easter.

"This is the worst day of my life," cried Maisie.

"Nope. Tomorrow's gonna be," said Honey.

"All because of a basket . . . a stupid, old basket!"

Honey buried her face in her hands. "No one's ever gonna believe Oxie knew a trick."

"Especially Glenda," said Maisie, crying louder. "Darn! If only we were talking to each other. Then I could borrow her basket."

They sat on the bottom of the basement steps, crying in unison. Then suddenly Honey popped her head out of her hands. "Hey! I'm still talking to Marshall. We can use his."

A quick phone call later, she was out the door, on her way to the Jaxes' house to borrow Marshall's basket. When she came back with it, Maisie checked to see if the handle was sturdy. It was. But she was still suspicious.

"Did Glenda *force* you to tell her why we needed it?"

"I didn't see Glenda."

"What about Marshall?"

"Marshall didn't care what it was for. He said we could use it as long as we liked." Honey tugged Maisie's arm. "C'mon. Let's go watch Oxie do his trick."

"Oxxiiieeeee!" called Maisie.

He heard her, but he stayed right where he was, with his head under her bed and the rest of his eighty-odd pounds stretched out behind him, in plain sight, on her beige carpet. No way was he leaving his hiding place! He'd had enough of those two girls!

"Oxxxiiieee!" Maisie called again, sounding closer.

He lay perfectly still, listening.

"Oh, *there* you are," she said a second later.

"Isn't that cute?" said Honey. "He thinks we can't see him."

Oxie cringed. Someone was feeling his rump.

"Oh, shoot . . . he's still damp," said Maisie. "We forgot to finish his grooming."

For the next half hour or so, she and Honey worked on Oxie, brushing and combing his tail and rear end with every intention of making him fit enough to win "Most Beautiful." While their blow dryer whirred, Lloyd's new rock album, *The Electric Octopus*, blasted down the hall from his room. He came out whistling to it on his way to take a shower.

Heyyy, heyyy, heyyy . . .
Know what I seen in the sea todayyy?

sang Pipe McGee, the rock star, as Lloyd stepped into the bathroom.

Maisie and Honey didn't hear the accident—

Lloyd had skidded across the slippery, wet tile floor, tripped over Honey's bedspread, then a clump of soaked towels, crashed into the sink, and conked his head—

or the yelling,

> . . . *I seen thee eee-lec-tric*
> *octo, octo puss . . .*

or any of the fuss their parents made when Lloyd showed them the mess the girls had left in the bathroom.

Mr. and Mrs. Blumm had a fit when they saw it and were on their way to Maisie's room just as Maisie fluffed up the tip of Oxie's tail and turned off her blow dryer.

"Okay, Oxie's all done," she said to Honey. "Now we can watch him carry his basket."

They never got the chance.

IT WAS nearly midnight when the two girls came out of the laundry room, staggering under the weight of the fourteen towels, bath mat, and bedspread they'd used on Oxie. For the last three hours, they'd mopped tiles, cleaned, loaded and unloaded the washer and dryer, folded towels, and cried.

Parents were so thick! Especially *their* parents. Neither of them would listen to reason. Oh, no. They had this dumb idea that nothing was more important than a safe bathroom. Not only safe, clean besides. And if Maisie and Honey didn't do it tonight, they couldn't go to the dog show.

They trudged upstairs, faced with the worst job of all—the bathtub. It was caked with thick dark rings of dog hair, dirt, dead fleas, and other unidentified insects.

Honey wept as she sprinkled it with cleanser. "You'd think old lazy Lloyd could've at least cleaned *this*!" she said. "Oxie's not just *ours*. He's *his* dog, too!"

She fell into bed as soon as the tub was scrubbed. But Maisie remembered her tube of E-Z BRONZE GEL. Worn out as she was, she took it out of her drawer and skimmed over the instructions:

APPLY LIGHT EVEN COAT. LEAVES SKIN WITH HEALTHY-LOOKING TAN OVERNIGHT. NO SUN NEEDED.

She didn't bother with the small print below:

Warning: Direct exposure to sun within twenty-four hours after application may result in dark blotches. *Avoid* heavy, uneven coat.

Maisie squirted the contents of the tube in her palm and slathered her face, her neck, her arms, and one kneecap before she ran out of gel. Oh, well. It didn't matter that she didn't have enough. Most of her would be tan for the dog show.

Then she got into bed, wearing her swim suit, and closed her eyes. Today was bad, she thought. But tomorrow is going to be wonderful.

⋅ Chapter 11 ⋅

HONEY was up. Lloyd was up. Mr. Blumm was flipping pancakes and Mrs. Blumm was pouring five glasses of orange juice when Maisie went down to the kitchen in the morning. On the radio was the weather report: unseasonably hot. In the high eighties and sunny all day. Like summer.

"Oh, goody!" Honey said, as she drowned a stack of pancakes in syrup. "Did you hear that, Maze? We can wear shorts to the dog show."

Maisie, who was disappointed that the gel hadn't worked, except to give her neck and arms a couple of small, pale freckles, sat down and spread a napkin across her lap. "I was already planning on it."

"Which ones?"

"My red Hawaiian shorts."

"Phone's ringing," said Mr. Blumm. "Somebody get it."

Honey popped up, grabbing it before Lloyd.

" 'Morning," she mumbled through a mouthful of pancakes. "This is the Blumm residence." Then she drummed her fingers impatiently on the counter. "Now, Marshall," she said, abruptly, "I can't understand you when you cry like that. Tell me again, okay? *Who* wrecked *who*? Glenda wrecked Snookums?"

Maisie was all ears as she drank her orange juice.

"She used *both*?" said Honey. "An electric razor *and* scissors?"

No one in the kitchen stirred.

"Did you try pasting it back on?"

Lloyd snickered and Honey shot him a dirty look.

"Laugh?" she said into the phone. "Of course nobody's gonna laugh, Marshall! Lots of dogs are bald. Millions. Just not around here, is all."

Lloyd nearly choked on a pancake and she turned her back to him, facing the spice rack on the wall above the counter.

"Sure, I'm sure," she told Marshall. "In fact, there's a king who won't *let* dogs in his country if they have one single hair on them! Where? Oh, uh . . . it's a place called . . . uh, Tarragon. T-A-R-R-A-G-O-N," she said, spelling the first label she saw in front of her. "That's right. Tarragon. So you stop crying and come to the show! You

hear? And you tell people that's where Snookums
is from. She's a *Tarragon terrier*."

Lloyd was practically blue when she hung up.

"Serves you right," she said, marching out of
the kitchen.

Maisie was behind her every step, asking about
Snookums. "What's happening? Is Glenda still
entering her in Most Beautiful?"

"Marshall didn't say," said Honey.

"But there's no point. If Glenda's shaved her,
she can't win anything."

"Oh, yes she can!"

"What for? She doesn't do tricks."

"For *Smallest* Dog in Deer Creek!"

WHEN the Blumms pulled in, there were easily
a hundred cars parked around the south end of
Baldwin Field, the place where the dog show was
being held.

"There's a spot down there, Daddy," said Honey.
"Look. In the next row."

She was sitting in the front with her parents,
holding the basket, and Maisie was jammed next
to the window in the back. Lloyd was on the other
side. Between them, taking up most of the seat,
was Oxie, panting.

Maisie stroked his clean, soft fur as she looked

out the window. Kids with dogs of every description were climbing out of cars, running and walking to get to the field. She knew some of the kids, but it was the dogs that held her interest. She saw a Rottweiler that looked as if it could chew logs, a wimpy shepherd, a peach-colored toy poodle, a black standard, three or four retrievers—golden and Lab—a squat, baggy-eyed Bloodhound, and more mixed breeds than she could count.

None of them could hold a candle to Oxie. Nope. Not one.

"See there, Oxie," she said, giving him a hug. "No doubt about it. You're the most beautiful dog in Deer Creek."

"That's what you think," said Lloyd. "Look back there."

"Oh, yeah! Where?" asked Maisie.

"Behind us," he said. "Getting out of that red Volvo."

Maisie whipped around to look out the rear window, but she couldn't see the car, the dog, or the boy who owned him until Mr. Blumm finished turning into their parking space. When she got out, she saw the boy first. "Why, that's Benedict . . . a kid who rides my bus," she said. Then her heart sank. She saw Benedict's dog.

He was pure white. Not cream, buff, ivory, or off-white, but pure, *sparkling* white. Standing in the sunlight, his long, heavy, well-brushed coat glistened. Shoot! He was perfect. He had a thick mane that could put a lion to shame. Upright, triangular ears. A nose like an ebony knob. And a tail that . . . Maisie bit her lip. She'd always thought Oxie's tail was the best in the world, but Benedict's dog's tail? Well, it was like a bouquet of snowy ostrich plumes.

Within moments, he'd drawn a crowd. Somebody was saying, "What a magnificent animal! What breed is he?" and somebody else was asking, "What's his name, son?"

"He's a Samoyed," Benedict said proudly. "And his name's Silver Chief."

"Never heard of one!" grumbled Honey.

Neither had Maisie, but it didn't matter. Silver Chief was the undisputed champion of beautiful dogs. The sure winner. She felt crushed and leaned down, whispering in Oxie's ear. "If you want to win a blue ribbon, you'd better do a *good* job carrying your basket."

Oxie wasn't listening. His eyes were rolling around in their sockets, following the movements of a butterfly that was fluttering over a car bumper. As the butterfly took off, he took off, dragging Maisie. "Whoooaaa . . . stop, Oxie!" she cried.

Like a miracle, it happened. Oxie stopped. But not because she'd told him to. He'd seen Amy Gooch's little golden Cocker spaniel and it was love at first sight. "Woof, woof, woof," he went, wagging his tail.

"Yap, yap, yap," went Amy's spaniel.

"Woof, woof, woof, woof!" answered Oxie.

Amy was acting annoyed and Maisie tried pulling Oxie away from them. "Come!" she commanded Oxie.

"He isn't very disciplined, is he?" said Amy.

Lloyd was thoroughly embarrassed, watching Maisie and Oxie make fools of themselves. "Here," he said, reaching for the leash. "Let *me* take him."

"No! *I'm* showing him," said Maisie.

Lloyd shrugged. "Okay, he's all yours, bimbo. Just don't tell anyone you're my sister."

He ran ahead, joining Mr. and Mrs. Blumm and Honey, who were crossing onto the field. Maisie coaxed Oxie to follow them, but he wouldn't move until Amy and her dog moved.

Amy sighed. "Goldie's a pedigreed Cocker spaniel. What's your dog? Some kind of collie mix?"

"Uh-uh. A pedigreed Tarragon husky. They're rare."

"Oh, right. I've heard of them," said Amy. "By the way, where's Glenda? You two fighting again?"

Maisie shook her head. "Nope. We're just not talking."

She was more than happy to reach the field.

In the sea of kids and dogs wandering around outside the ring, it was easy to shake Amy and Goldie. The ring itself had been put up earlier that morning. It was a makeshift circle of slim stakes poked in the ground every ten feet or so, then linked together with a single stream of yellow plastic ribbon. On one side was an entrance. Facing it, on the other side, was a table with three chairs set up, inside the ring, for the judges.

A judge in a green baseball cap was already announcing over a bullhorn that it was time for the dogs competing in the Smallest Dog category to line up by the entrance with their owners.

Maisie stretched her neck, looking for Glenda. She and Snookums didn't seem to be there. "Come!" she said to Oxie. He wouldn't budge. He'd seen a little girl in an umbrella stroller, eating a box of animal crackers.

The little girl giggled as Oxie sat squarely in front of her, raising his paw. "Doggie begging," she said, handing him a cracker. While Oxie chomped on it, Maisie led him to the spot where her parents, Lloyd, and Honey were standing, close behind the yellow ribbon. Lloyd moved away when he saw her.

"Where's the basket?" she asked Honey.

"Down there," Honey said, pointing to the grass in back of her.

"Will the dogs in the first category please enter

the ring with their owners?" called the judge with the bullhorn.

In they came, one by one, the littlest dogs in Deer Creek. Beside each dog was its owner wearing a cardboard tag with a number. Number 17, the first to enter, was a teenage girl walking a black-and-white Jack Russell terrier. Next came a pug, followed by a yellow Pekingese, then a Shih tzu, a Dachshund mix, a corgi, a shelti, the peach-colored poodle Maisie had seen earlier, another Shih tzu only much prettier, then a . . .

Oh, no! *Was it?* That ridiculous-looking sheared thing with a big pink bow and stiff, spiked tufts along its spine? Snookums had a *Mohawk!*

"Here they come, guys!" cried Honey. "They're Number Nine!"

Maisie fanned the air as they paraded by. Snookums smelled to high heaven. She was wearing Old Spice after-shave. And her nails were painted!

Mr. Blumm could hardly click his camera. Tears were streaming down his face and Mrs. Blumm's shoulders were shaking. "Stop laughing . . . *both* of you!" Honey whispered. Then she nudged Maisie. "Did you see that? Her nose? How dark it was?"

Maisie's mouth was still open. "Snookums's nose was always dark," she said.

"Not Snookums's nose! *Glenda's!*"

Maisie looked again. It was too late. All she could see was Glenda's backside. And she was wearing *her* Hawaiian shorts.

"Boys, girls, ladies and gentlemen . . . our decision is in," called the judge with the bullhorn. "The winner of the Smallest Dog category is . . ."

Even the dogs were quiet as he held up a score card.

"Nummm-ber Nine! I repeat! Nummm-ber Nine! Snookums! A, uh, I believe this says . . ." He paused, holding the card farther from his face. "Yes, it does!" he shouted. "A Tarragon terrier! Weighing three pounds, fourteen ounces and shown by its owner, Miss Glenda Jax!"

There was a roar of applause and a few loud whistles as Glenda and Snookums ran back to the ring to accept their ribbon.

Honey was jumping up and down, screaming, "It worked, it worked, it worked!"

Mr. Blumm kept clicking his camera and Maisie squinted, trying to get a good look at Glenda's nose. It really was dark . . . like a barbeque coal.

All three judges were shaking Glenda's hand. She smiled and clipped the blue ribbon to her shirt. One judge in a big, wide skirt was bending down to pat Snookums.

Up until then, Oxie had been unusually quiet, lying on the grass by Maisie's feet. When he recognized his Poppin Road neighbors, he rose to his haunches, greeting them with his deepest woof, woof, woofs. Then he lay back down again, continuing with the pastime that was keeping him quiet.

Maisie and Honey didn't notice. They were too busy watching the town's jumbo dogs line up for the next category.

"I think the shiny black Great Dane's gonna win," said Honey.

"I don't. The St. Bernard's bigger," said Maisie.

"Bet you a quarter."

The sun was beating down on them so hard, Maisie stretched her T-shirt away from her neck and blew between her collar bones.

"No, thank you. I don't gamble," she said.

If she had, she wouldn't have lost money. An Irish wolfhound, big enough to saddle, took first place. Coming in second was an overweight Newfoundland, drooling silvery strings of saliva.

Boy, it was hot!

The jumbo dogs were hardly out of the ring when the judge with the bullhorn called for the owners of dogs competing in the Best Trick category to come get their number cards.

Honey grinned. "Okay, Maisie, that's us," she said, reaching for the basket she thought was behind her. "Hey!" Her fingers wiggled in the air. "Where's Marshall's basket?"

RRRrrriiippp!!!

Their eyes met with the most horrible sight either of them ever could have imagined. Oxie's jaws were grinding up the handle. It was off. Completely off. The six-inch, frayed part sticking out of his mouth looked like the leafy end of a stalk of celery.

"You scuzz! You bum! You cockroach! You, you, you . . ."

Honey's tantrum was so bad, Mrs. Blumm had to drag her, kicking and screaming, out to the car.

Lloyd threw what was left of the basket into a trash barrel and took Oxie for a walk. Maisie stayed by her dad's side at the ring, crying silently into his hankie.

She'd *never* get over this. Never! She hated dog shows. She hated dogs. Life stunk. Her only comforting thought was that nothing—ever again—would match the nightmare of seeing that basket.

"It's totally wrecked, Daddy. We'll have to buy Marshall a new one," she said, wiping her wet cheeks.

Mr. Blumm nodded. "We will, sugar. We'll take it out of Oxie's allowance."

As rotten as Maisie felt, she laughed at her dad's joke. Then she looked out in the ring and started crying all over again. None of the tricks that the dogs in the Best Trick category were doing were anything special. A few dogs sat. One rolled over. Another fetched a ball. Goldie, Amy Gooch's Cocker spaniel, won the blue ribbon for doing nothing better than hopping three times on her hind legs to get a Cheez Doodle.

After Amy shook the judges' hands and left the ring, Maisie saw Glenda, with her strange, dark nose, go over to Amy and congratulate her. She bit her lip and her dad asked her if she wanted to go home.

Maisie shook her head. "I can't. I'll look like a poor sport. I'm going to stay and watch Benedict show Silver Chief in Most Beautiful."

"They're giving the last call for it right now," said Mr. Blumm. "Sure you don't want to show Oxie? He might win second."

"Nope. He won't. The shiny black Great Dane will."

"Third place, maybe?"

"Uh-uh," said Maisie. "The pretty Shih tzu's going to win third."

She was right. That was the exact order in which the three dogs placed.

"Attention! May I please have your attention?" called the judge with the bullhorn. "Coming up next is the fifth and final category of the Deer Creek Dog Show. Owners of dogs competing for Most Intelligent, please get your number cards."

As Maisie listened, she saw Lloyd coming back from his walk with Oxie. Oxie was straining at his leash to get to the trash barrel, and Lloyd was pulling the other way, trying to keep him from it.

Typical. Absolutely typical, she thought. Whatever stubborn old Oxie is supposed to do, he does just the opposite. Jerk his leash one way, he goes the other. It was something you could always count on with Oxie. That's why he looked dumb. He never obeyed. To make him look smart, she'd have to . . . *of course*! She'd have to tell him to do what *he* wanted to do!

Suddenly she found herself wiping her nose and smiling. She had a plan.

"Daddy, guess what?" she said. "I'm entering Oxie in this category."

"In Most *Intelligent*?"

"That's right," she said, handing him his hankie.

She left her father looking as if he'd been stunned by a brick and ran to meet Lloyd. Lloyd didn't know what she was up to, so he was more than willing to turn Oxie over to her. But first he had a comment. "You're getting a weird tan . . . like *really* weird."

Right then, Maisie couldn't have cared less. "Never mind. Just give me Oxie's leash," she told him.

"Okay, here. Go ahead . . . take him," said Lloyd. "But I'm warning you, you'll never get him away from this trash barrel."

"Oh, yeah? Watch. *Stay, Oxie!*" she ordered.

As soon as Oxie heard the command, he took off like a rocket.

Maisie was out of breath when they got to the ring entrance. About eight or nine dogs and their owners were already waiting there, including Goldie and Amy. She steered clear of Amy and went directly to a woman with short, gray hair who was handing out number cards.

"My dog isn't signed up for this," panted Maisie. "But I've changed my mind . . . I want to enter him. Is it all right?"

The woman gave her an odd look, but nodded. "You're in the nick of time," she said. "Give me your name, your dog's name, and your dog's breed."

"Maisie Blumm with two *m*'s. His name's Oxie. And he's uh, oh, a *mutt*!"

Mixed breed, the woman wrote on a pad. "Okey-dokey, dear, you're all set. Here's your number card and good luck," she said, looking down at Oxie.

Number nine. The same card Glenda had. As Maisie pinned it to her shirt, she felt someone tap her arm. She turned and saw Marshall.

"I thought Oxie was s'posed to be in Best Trick," he said.

"He was, but . . . well, Marshall. I don't know how to tell you this. I'm sorry, but, well . . . your basket got wrecked."

"That's okay," he said, following her to the place where the other dogs were waiting. "It wasn't mine, anyway. It was Glenda's. Where's Honey?"

"*Glenda's?* I mean, Honey? Out in our car. Mom had to take her there . . . she was having a tantrum."

Marshall didn't ask why. He was off and running toward the parking lot.

The Most Intelligent category was already in progress. The first dog, a German shepherd, was sitting about ten yards from its owner, a boy Lloyd's age. The boy whistled and the dog trotted over to him. "*Paw!*" The dog pawed. "*Jump!*" The dog jumped. "*Come!*" The dog came.

There was a nice round of applause as the two left the ring. Now Amy and Goldie were going out there. And wouldn't you just know it? They were doing that Cheez Doodle thing again.

Out of the corner of her eye, Maisie saw Glenda standing with her parents and a bunch of other people. Glenda was looking at Maisie. Staring. And she was *laughing*!

So, she thought it was funny, huh? Oxie competing in Most Intelligent. Maisie'd show her!

"Number Nine?" someone asked.

Maisie looked down at a little girl missing two teeth.

"You wanna take my place? I'm next. But I have to go to the bathroom."

"Yeah, sure. I'll switch," said Maisie. "You'll be last then."

"You got spots," said the little girl.

Maisie didn't hear. Her heart was pounding like a kettledrum. Amy and Goldie were finishing, and it was time for her and Oxie. She jerked his leash. "Stay!" she said to get him going. He flew through the entrance, but from that moment on, Maisie knew she had to give orders that made him *look* like he was obeying.

That was her plan: To tell him to do *exactly* what he wanted to do. And right now, he wanted to see Goldie.

"*Go over to the little doggie coming out of the ring!*" she hollered so everybody at the dog show could hear.

Oxie ran over to Goldie.

"*Sniff the doggie all over!*" she ordered.

Oxie sniffed and sniffed Goldie.

"*Now say hello to her!*"

"Woof, woof woof," went Oxie.

"*Wag your tail!*"

From side to side it went, like a windshield wiper.

So far, so good, thought Maisie. But there was trouble ahead. Oxie was going to want to follow Goldie out of the ring. What now? How could she stop him?

Aha! Just what they needed. A fly was buzzing

past her right foot. She jerked Oxie's leash to the left. He felt the jerk and pulled right.

"*Turn right!*" she shouted.

He was already turning. Terrific. Now he saw the fly.

"*Follow that fly!*" she ordered.

Hi ho and away he went, galloping after it.

"Wow! Look at that!" shouted somebody at ringside. "That dog's *really* following a fly!"

They were nearly up to the yellow ribbon on the other side of the ring. Straight ahead, just behind the ribbon, was the little girl in the umbrella stroller. Oxie suddenly lost interest in the fly. Maisie knew he'd seen the animal crackers.

"*Stop right where you are!*" she commanded.

Oxie squealed to a halt a foot in front of the little girl.

"*Sit and paw!*"

He sat and pawed, begging for a cracker. The little girl knew it and held one up.

"*What a nice little girl! She wants to give you a cracker. Take it!*"

Oxie already had it in his mouth.

"*Now eat it!*"

Chomp, chomp.

"*Thump your tail to thank the little girl!*"

Thump, thump, thump went Oxie's tail.

He wasn't thanking anybody. He was begging

for another cracker. Maisie knew it, but the people watching didn't, and they went wild, clapping. Shoot! She'd never get him away now.

"*Okay! Time for a game of Tug of War!*" she hollered.

Oxie strained at his leash, pulling toward the animal crackers, and Maisie dug her heels in the ground, pulling toward the center of the ring.

"*Harder! Tug harder!*" she shouted.

Darn it. He was. He was going to knock her flat on her face.

"*That's it! Try and beat me!*"

Just then, the fly buzzed by again, hovering over Oxie's nose. He stopped pulling when he saw it.

"*Stop! Game's over!*" Maisie yelled, watching the fly buzz left. "*Now make a turn to your left!*" she ordered.

Oxie was already going that way, dead set on catching the fly.

"Well, I'll be!" shouted an old man. "That dog knows his right from his left!"

The fly flew higher. "*Leap!*" called Maisie.

Oxie leaped in the air after the fly.

"*Straight!*" called Maisie when she saw the fly going straight. "*Go straight, Oxie!*"

He did, following the fly in a straight path right out of the ring.

♦ ♦ ♦

MAISIE didn't have a chance to enjoy all the clapping and cheering. As soon as she and Oxie got out of the ring, they were swamped by people who'd come to congratulate them.

Kids were edging in to pet Oxie. Cameras were clicking. One man was asking Maisie if she and her dog were interested in making a commercial.

"Excuse me, sir. I was talking to her first," said a woman with curly red hair and a scratchy voice. She flashed him a card that said she was a newspaper reporter, then turned to Maisie. "I'd like to write a little story about you, honey. What's your name?"

Maisie was bent over, gaping at her kneecaps. "Maisie Blumm with two m's."

"Well, now, Maisie. How did you go about training your dog to do all the wonderful things he did?"

Maisie quickly slapped her hand over her blotchy, brown kneecap. "It was just a matter of really getting to know him."

"Hey! Don't forget! He's *my* dog, too!" said Honey, suddenly bursting in on the scene. "I helped train him." She poked the woman. "Wanna talk to me?"

Marshall crowded in next to Honey. "And me?" he asked. "I'm the dog's neighbor."

"And I'm the *owner's* best friend," said Glenda, using her elbows to push past them.

"Boys, girls, ladies and gentlemen. Our decision is in," called the judge with the bullhorn. "The winner of the Most Intelligent Dog in Deer Creek is Nummm-ber Nine! I repeat! Nummmber Nine. Oxie! A mix . . ."

He was interrupted by so much clapping and loud catcalls, he had to wait to go on.

". . . mixed breed shown by its owner, Miss Maisie Blumm!"

As she heard her name, Maisie was making a discovery. She was covered with huge brown blotches.

"Get out there . . . get your ribbon," said Glenda.

"I can't. Look at me!"

"Stop being a jerk, you dope! Who's gonna look at *you?* They want to see Oxie," Glenda said, pushing her through the crowd toward the entrance.

Oxie bolted forward. Someone he knew was coming out to the center of the ring, and he was dying to get to her. Maisie squinted to see who it was. *Rosemary Hall*! The dogcatcher! *She* was the judge in the big, wide skirt.

Oxie kissed Rosemary's hands, her feet, her legs and sniffed her all over as the judge with the bullhorn congratulated Maisie. Maisie mumbled thank you, then held her hand out to the next judge. Oh, oh!

"Still painting your face and body, huh?" said Mr. Abruzzio, the owner of the Downtown Deli.

Maisie smiled sheepishly as he clipped the blue ribbon on her shirt.

Blast it! Now she had to face Rosemary. Rosemary laughed as she reached out to hug her. "Know what I think?" she whispered. "This prize ought to be for Most Intelligent *kid* in town!"

Oxie was up on his hind legs, licking Rosemary's face, and she was scratching behind his ears. He hadn't fooled her. No way. But he'd fooled nearly everybody else at the dog show.

The clapping and cheering wouldn't end.

"LIKE I still can't believe it," Lloyd said for the three millionth time as Mr. Blumm pulled their car into the driveway.

"Believe it!" snapped Honey, who was sick and tired of hearing him. "Oxie's smart! I always knew he was."

She was first out of the car and ran up to the mailbox. "Hey, Maisie. You got a letter."

Maisie was watching Glenda get out of the Jaxes' blue station wagon across the street. "Yeah? Who's it from?"

"P. Whittelsey. It's from Rome."

"Rome! Did you say *Rome*!" she screeched.

"Heyyy, Glenda! Get over here quick! My balloon went to *Rome*!"

While she tore up to the mailbox, Glenda dashed across the street to meet her. Side by side they went into the house and up the stairs with their arms around each other.

Maisie laughed. "How come only your nose got blotched?"

"That's the only place I put the gel. I wanted to look like a skiier."

"Boy, do we have a lot to put in *The Poppin Road Gazette*."

Glenda agreed. "We sure do," she said. "Let's make the next edition totally about the dog show."

When they got to the landing, they apologized and made up. Maisie said she was sorry Oxie chewed up Glenda's basket and Glenda said it was perfectly all right. She'd wanted a bigger basket anyway.

Then they promised they'd never, ever fight again. Ever. They swore to it.

"You're the very best friend I ever had," said Glenda.

"And you're mine," said Maisie.

Then they hugged and went inside her room to read her letter, certain that nothing would ever come between them again.

14 Buffalo Hill Ave.
Rome, New York

Dear Maisie,

   *I bet never in your life did you think your balloon
would go so far away as a place like New York, did
you? I found it this morning on our woodpile when I
was chasing my duck Betty around our yard. Me and
my sisters have three and they're all pets but we keep
them penned up, the ducks I mean. Betty gets out
though, all the time. The air was mostly gone from
the balloon, so at first I thought it was an apple.
Then I saw the letter tied to it.*

   *You couldn't have picked a better person to tell
about your jerky friend Glenda. I knew just how you
felt. She sounds sooo much like my friend Peggy Jo
who's always teasing and saying cats are better than
having dumb, quacking ducks. She's got four. Cats,
that is, and a hermit crab. Talk about dumb, try
crabs.*

   *I guess you must be saying, who is this writing to
me? My name's Trish Whittelsey, but on my birth cer-
tificate it says Patricia Lynn Whittelsey and I'm
eleven, or I will be next week. I was going to tell you
my hair is brown, but Mom says it's chestnut, so my
eyes must be chestnut too because they're brown. I'm
five feet one already. We grow big quick in our
house. Kathleen is twelve and her feet are size 10,
but not for long. Her duck is Bill. My other sister is*

fourteen and her duck is Suzy and she's Angie and she weighs over a hundred thirty (my sister I'm talking about). I know this because we have doctor's scales and when you step off, the weight's still there. Angie lies and says she's only a hundred six. She talks on the phone so much, me and Kathleen tell people she's not in when they call even if she is. We couldn't ever use the phone if we didn't.

I'm not sure yet what I want to be when I grow up unless it's an astronaut if they take big astronauts. Maybe I'll own a dress shop with Peggy Jo if we're still friends then, which we might not be because we're always fighting, over ducks mostly, but sometimes it's about her belching. I can't eat lunch when she does it.

My dad's an osteopath which is like a doctor and that's why we have doctor's scales. My mom has stationery that says Dorothy M. Whittelsey, Ph.D. H.M. and it means doctor of home management. My Grandma Rose lives with us and in some other letter I'll tell you about her girdles and the funny toothbrush she uses to get food out of her gums.

I'm sure your dog Oxie will win for most beautiful. He sounds much, much prettier than Glenda's hairy mouse. That was a funny picture you drew of her.

Write back to me soon. Your friend from Rome,

Trish
Whittelsey

DEER CREEK'S CHAMPION DOGS

SmALLEst

Bzzzz

MoSt INTELLiGENT